FATAL CONSPIRACY

KATIE METTNER

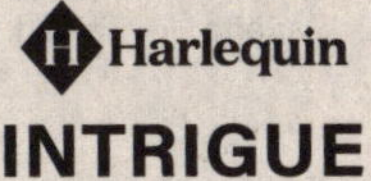

INTRIGUE

For Kisber. My sister, my friend.

Recycling programs for this product may not exist in your area.

ISBN-13: 978-1-335-18910-3

Fatal Conspiracy

For questions and comments about the quality of this book, please contact us at CustomerService@Harlequin.com.

Harlequin Enterprises ULC
22 Adelaide St. West, 41st Floor
Toronto, Ontario M5H 4E3, Canada
www.Harlequin.com

HarperCollins Publishers
Macken House, 39/40 Mayor Street Upper,
Dublin 1, D01 C9W8, Ireland
www.HarperCollins.com

Printed in Lithuania

1 2 3 4 5 6 7 8 9 10 LIT 28 27 26 25

"I don't use the walker unless I'm injured or sick.

"Now it's just a requirement on remote jobs in case something happens."

"Like you get dropped from an SUV by thugs looking for the guy you were just trying to help."

Alayah tossed Derek a wink. "Just like that. Now let's get this hunt for a killer underway. I'm sure you'd like to clear your name sooner rather than later and return to your life in..." She waited for him to fill in the blank.

"Minneapolis," he answered. "But I'd be lying if I said I was looking forward to returning to that life. When we left Minneapolis a few days ago, I already knew I'd outgrown my time there."

Alayah thought about what he'd said. Was she happy with her life? Would she want to change anything if the opportunity arose? The answer was obvious, but the path to love wasn't navigable for her. She'd have to find fulfillment in her work and leave the world of love behind.

Katie Mettner wears the title of "the only person to lose her leg after falling down the bunny hill" and loves decorating her prosthetic leg to fit the season. She lives in Northern Wisconsin with her own happily-ever-after and spends the day writing romantic stories with her sweet puppy by her side. Katie has an addiction to coffee and dachshunds and a lessening aversion to Pinterest—now that she's quit trying to make the things she pins.

Books by Katie Mettner

Harlequin Intrigue

Secure Watch

Dark Web Investigation
Tracing Her Stolen Identity
Deadly Security Breach
Fatal Conspiracy

Secure One

Going Rogue in Red Rye County
The Perfect Witness
The Red River Slayer
The Silent Setup
The Masquerading Twin
Holiday Under Wraps

Visit the Author Profile page at Harlequin.com.

CAST OF CHARACTERS

Alayah Heath—Alayah is new to Secure Watch but isn't new to the ways of Silicon Valley. She's trusted to lead the on-site cybersecurity team at a conference of tech bros in Duluth, Minnesota. As a little person, she's faced challenges proving herself among ex-military men, so she jumps at the chance. When she witnesses a murder on her first day, she worries she should have looked before she leaped.

Derek Benjamin—He has a decision to make: remain Hugo Victor's assistant and run himself ragged for someone else, or venture out on his own. He plans to decide over a plate of fresh lake trout at his cabin—until he's accused of murdering his boss.

Hugo Victor—When the owner of Black Marlin Productions collapses onstage in front of thousands, he leaves behind a labyrinth of hatred that runs deeper than Lake Superior. Who hated him enough to kill him so publicly?

Josh Hunt—The owner of Virtual Scorpion Productions has been nothing but green with envy since he was asked to leave Black Marlin Productions years ago. Now, he'd love to get a little payback. The question is, would he go as far as murder?

The Board of Black Marlin Productions—They've tried to pass a vote of no confidence on Hugo before. Did they finally succeed in the most permanent way possible?

Chapter One

The lights of Whiplash, the small town Alayah Heath called home, appeared in the distance, and she let out a sigh of relief. After working on-site for the last week, she was exhausted and ready to spend a few nights sleeping in her own bed. Once she'd helped her employer Secure Watch install new computer equipment at a business in St. Paul, she'd stayed behind to teach their tech team how to use the new equipment with their cloud and keep their data safe. Overall, Alayah was confident they would be fine, but she would check in with them next week to see if they had questions after using the new equipment with their software.

It had been a long day of travel, made longer by the fact that, as a little person, she required hand controls to drive. At a hair under four feet tall, there was no way her feet were reaching the pedals of the fleet SUV, but thankfully, her custom booster seat gave her enough height to see out the windshield. She had been diagnosed with Ellis-Van Creveld syndrome at birth, a type of dwarfism that left her with short forearms and lower leg bones, as well as other skeletal abnormalities. Her birth parents hadn't stuck around long when they learned the extent of her condition, but a wonderful couple adopted her as a baby. They were there through all the surgeries and therapy, and she knew how lucky she was to have them.

After working for several companies in California, she was never more grateful that Secure Inc.—which encompassed her employer, Secure Watch, along with the personal security company, Secure One—had many people with disabilities working for them, so their approach to accessibility came from personal experience. Several of the fleet vehicles had hand controls, and she was grateful to be independent while working offsite.

When Alayah left Silicon Valley four years ago to work for Secure Watch, she hadn't known what to expect, but she knew she was ready for a change. Her new boss, Mina Jacobs, was disabled and had built a thriving business by understanding everyone's strengths and weaknesses and playing to them. That was something she'd never experienced in the workplace before.

Happy to be home, she pulled down the lane onto the property that housed Secure Inc. and stopped at the security booth. When Cal Newfellow, the owner of Secure Inc., had first bought the property, it was nothing like what it was now, which was essentially a fortress to protect those who protected others.

"Hey, Alayah," Zac, one of the Secure One guards, who also worked for Secure Watch when needed, greeted her. "Nice to see you. We were getting worried you might need an assist."

"Sorry," she said, instantly feeling bad for worrying them. "There was a lot of construction, which added to the drive time. I'm ready to call it a night, though."

"I bet you are," Zac said. "I'll ring Mina and let her know you're back. She wants to speak with you."

Alayah brushed her hand at him. "I have nothing thrilling to report. The briefing can wait until tomorrow."

"It's not about that," he said, pushing a button for the gate to open. "She needs your help with something else. She said she'd be waiting in the cafeteria with a plate of your favorite cookies and a hot chocolate."

Her groan turned into laughter, which made Zac laugh, too. "She does know my weaknesses!"

"The only ones you have, if you ask anyone here," Zac said, waving as she smiled and slipped the SUV through the gate before it closed again. When she pulled into the garage, the new Secure Inc. hire was waiting to help her down, so she didn't need the small step stool she carried with her when driving larger vehicles.

"Thanks, Jonah," she said, stretching her back.

"My pleasure, Alayah. I'll unload the equipment and put your suitcase at your door. You've been summoned."

"So I've heard," she agreed, shaking her head as she took her purse from him. "At least there will be cookies." She headed into the hallway, winding her way through the main building that housed their offices, control rooms, some employee quarters and the cafeteria.

The lodge, as Cal called it, had been added on to multiple times over the years, and the property behind it was now dotted with cabins where married couples from the team lived. With more than forty on-site employees, the need for housing was always changing and increasing, but so far, Cal had been able to keep up with the demand. It helped that many of the Secure Watch employees worked remotely or lived in other parts of the state to support different regions.

The first time Alayah had walked into the cafeteria, she'd turned around and walked right back out, only to be snagged by their resident cook and nanny, Sadie Newman. She was married to Eric, a Secure One operative, and they were now the proud parents of a little boy. Sadie still cooked three meals a day for the entire crew and took great offense at people turning their noses up at her cooking. At least, that was the joke Sadie had used that day when she found Alayah fighting back tears in the hallway.

Why did she have such a visceral reaction to a cafeteria? It reminded her of elementary school, where she was teased mercilessly for being short and using a walker. Not one teacher or adult in the school attempted to stop the bullies or educate them about disabilities. That hurt as much as the teasing did. The bullying had left deep scars that were easy to irritate, even years later. Sadie had sweetly reminded her that no one in the building teased anyone about anything, and all were welcome. Sadie had led her back in, where she found a special chair waiting to help her reach the table. That was when she understood she was accepted and welcomed at Secure Inc.

"Alayah!" a little voice said, and she glanced up to see Mina's daughter, Hannah Grace, barreling toward her from the cafeteria. Hannah was only four, but Alayah still had to brace herself for her exuberant hugs.

"Hi, sweetheart," she said, hugging the little girl. "You've grown since I was gone. You're almost taller than I am! I'm pretty short, though."

Hannah giggled and slipped her hand into hers. "You're silly. You're not short. You're petite. That's what Dad says."

"Well, your dad is quite kind," she said with a smile. "Isn't it past your bedtime?"

"It is," Mina said, standing when she saw them walk in. "But Roman is in a meeting, and since I also needed to speak with you, I told her she could stay up until we're done."

Sitting, Alayah frowned. "I'm sorry to hold you up. Construction traffic was bad."

"You know what they say about Minnesota. There are only two seasons. Construction and winter."

They laughed as she helped herself to a cookie and dunked it in her hot cocoa while Hannah Grace did the same. They giggled and clinked cookies before taking a giant bite.

"Zac said you needed to talk to me about something," she said when she finished chewing. "I hope I didn't do anything wrong."

"Of course not," Mina said, waving in dismissal. "It's just that time is of the essence with this situation. The convention crew at a hotel in Duluth contacted us today. They're holding a tech conference and had planned to run the entire thing themselves until they were notified that Hugo Victor would be there."

Alayah raised an eyebrow. "*The* Hugo Victor?"

"Yep," Mina agreed with a nod. "He had originally said no, but they went to the bargaining table, and he finally agreed. Turns out he has a new app he wants to promote. Anyway, with him, as well as several other big-name tech gurus from your old stomping grounds, coming in for the conference, the convention decided they'd be spread too thin. They'd like us to come in and manage the tech equipment while Secure One manages the personal safety of the speakers and guests."

"Easy enough. I can help you get everything prepped for that tomorrow." Alayah paused, remembering information that had come across her desk about a tech conference in

Duluth. "Wait. I thought that particular convention started on Thursday."

"It does," Mina said, biting her lower lip.

"As in two days from now Thursday?"

"Yep," Mina agreed. "It's extremely short notice, and I know we promise that you'll get a few days off after a job like you just finished, but I need you on this, Alayah."

"Who's running point on it? I'll get with them to see how I can help fill in holes."

"Well, if you agree, that would be you."

Mina wanted her to run point on a conference of this size? That was both flattering and anxiety-inducing, not to mention a lot to ask of one person in this kind of setting.

"Cal will have us covered for the security aspect, but I don't have a full team to spare for this. We're currently juggling too many other jobs. Cal plans to send Declan and Zac, who can pull double duty for Secure Watch and Secure One, but you'd be point for the cybersecurity aspect and equipment. You're familiar with the tech moguls attending, so you'll have insight into how best to approach the cybersecurity and the personal security situations. Cal's team would appreciate any help you can give them with that as well. It's a lot to ask, but I need you."

Alayah nodded. "That's not a problem, Mina. I'll reset everything tomorrow morning and head back to Duluth with the team to prepare."

Mina's face contorted again, and Alayah suspected that what she was about to say wasn't for the weak of heart. "They need you there in the morning."

"You want us to go *tonight*?"

With a nod, Mina patted her arm. "I can tell you're exhausted, so I hate asking. Had I known sooner, I would have had you stop in Duluth on your way here, but we just got off the planning call with them. The equipment is ready and the Secure One guys are loading everything. You don't have to drive, either. We've got you booked into the hotel, but there is a mandatory meeting at eight a.m."

She did some fast math in her head. They'd get to Duluth around 11:00 p.m., but if she slept on the way there and through the night, she'd be rested by morning. "Tomorrow is just a setup and meeting day?"

"Yes, so there will be plenty of downtime for you to rest before the convention begins."

"Sounds fine then. If the guys can give me ten minutes to pack a new suitcase, I'm in."

"Thank you," Mina said with a sigh. "I'd go, but they need me here for two other jobs. You're a lifesaver."

"As long as I don't have to drive, I'm up for it," she promised. "Do you have the specs I need to know before the morning meeting?"

Mina held up her finger and pulled out her phone. She hit a button, and in seconds, Alayah's phone beeped. "You own it. Take your time and read it over during the drive. Message me with any questions. You're sure you're okay with this?"

The short glimpse of the email told her that her sleeping time in the car had just evaporated, but she nodded anyway. They were a team at Secure Inc., so she would step up and do her part. Besides, she'd never had the opportunity to be the point person on a huge event such as this, which meant she'd earned her stripes at Secure Watch. She smiled, knowing that the little voice in her head that said she'd never be good enough was now silenced for good.

"Completely okay with it. If it's important to you and Cal, it's important to me."

Alayah hugged Hannah Grace and waved as she left the

cafeteria, the relief on her boss's face telling her she'd made the right call. Mina didn't need to tell her what a successful convention like this would mean for Secure Inc. It would likely garner them more work than they could ever handle without growing exponentially, which no one was averse to. First, though, she had to do her job and do it well, so she rolled her suitcase through the door of her room to repack. Home sweet home would have to wait just a little bit longer.

Chapter Two

Derek Benjamin was buzzing with excitement. His boss, Hugo Victor of Black Marlin Technologies, was scheduled to open the tech conference in less than an hour. Once he was onstage, Derek would be on his way to his cabin for a much-needed few days of rest and relaxation. Well, he'd get some relaxation time, but he'd also be working. There was no such thing as time off when you took the position as Hugo Victor's assistant. However, it was still the first time he wouldn't be connected to Hugo at the hip in over a year.

He glanced around the room, searching for the man he was told would meet him there, but the only other person in the room was a she. Her back was to him, but she had long, wavy brown hair curling at the tips that hung nearly to her waist. He did a doubletake when he realized she was a child, and she must be lost.

"Can I help you find someone?" he asked, worried she was looking for her mom or dad.

When she turned, he took a step back to see that she was a woman and not a child. "I'm not lost, are you?"

"Na—no," he stuttered, waiting for his mouth to catch up with his brain. He noticed her name badge. "Alayah. That's a pretty name."

"Thanks," she said, her smile bright as her blue eyes

sparkled. "You even pronounced it correctly, so points for that. And you are?"

"Derek Benjamin," he said, stretching his hand out to her. "I'm Hugo Victor's assistant. I was told to meet someone named Cal Newfellow here, so when you turned around, it caught me by surprise."

She slipped her hand into his to offer a firm handshake, even though his hand easily swallowed hers. "Cal is around here somewhere. I came in looking for coffee so I can keep my eyes open for the next few hours."

"That's in the room across the hall," he said, pointing to his left after he dropped her hand. He couldn't help but think she had great energy, and he would love to get to know her better. Too bad he was leaving. "Secure Watch," he said, reading her badge. "Is that a super-secret spy organization?"

Alayah's laughter filled the room, making him smile. He'd expected tinkling bells but got a lilting hee-haw that ended in a giggle. "It wouldn't be very super-secret spy-ish of me to walk around wearing my name on my chest, would it?"

"True, true," he agreed, still grinning. "I'm kidding, though. I've heard nothing but good things about your company. In fact, I was relieved to hear Secure One and Secure Watch would be here protecting the conference."

"We were a last-minute addition, but I assure you, we'll do everything possible to ensure the conference goes off without a hitch. To that end, I'd better return to my station and prepare for sound check."

He bowed and stepped out of the way of the door. "It was nice to meet you, Alayah from Secure Watch. Don't forget the coffee. You'll need it if you're forced to sit through my boss's speech."

She laughed again, which was precisely what he wanted. "I used to work in Silicon Valley, so I'm quite familiar with your boss's penchant for long-winded discourse. Come to think of it, maybe I'll get a pot and a straw."

He smiled at the image it evoked. "It would save you a trip at hour two of his presentation." Alayah grimaced, and he laughed. "I'm kidding. He should wrap it up in an hour and fifty-seven minutes. There's a reason I'm leaving for a little R and R the moment he takes the stage. I've heard him speak no less than two hundred times, so I think I'll pass on this one."

"Can't blame you there," she agreed. "Besides, there's no better place than Duluth for some R and R."

That was one thing they both agreed on. "Have you seen someone named Cal Newfellow? That's who I'm supposed to find."

"Cal should be along any minute. You can't miss him. He's wearing a Secure One shirt, a name badge, and is sporting some fancy apparatus." She waggled the fingers on her right hand and then left the room.

He stared after her, still wearing a goofy grin. What an unexpected bright spot she was on this day! A man walked through the door, but Derek didn't need to see his shirt to know Cal Newfellow had arrived. When he extended his right hand, he indeed wore a fancy prosthesis to replace his missing fingers.

"You must be Derek," he said. "I'm Cal Newfellow."

Derek shook his hand with a nod. "I am, and it's very nice to meet you. They told me you would be the one to take Hugo's things to the stage."

"Yes, I'm happy to get it set up while you attend to your boss," Cal agreed, accepting the water bottle and other supplies he handed off.

"I appreciate it. I'm needed backstage but let me know if you have any questions."

Cal held up the bottle with a smile. "In my old job, I drove diplomats through the streets of Kabul during air raids."

"So, you're saying you can handle a water bottle without question. Probably a fair assessment," he said, laughing at himself. "It seems I've put my foot in it several times in the last few minutes."

"Assumed Alayah was a lost child?" Cal asked, still not cracking a smile.

"Yep," he admitted. "In fairness, she had her back turned to me when I walked in." Cal was about to say something else when Derek's name was called over the loudspeaker, asking him to return to the back of the stage. "Looks like Hugo's patience has run out. Thanks for your help, Cal." He waved and beat it out of Dodge before he put his other foot in his mouth.

In record time, he was standing backstage in front of his boss. "I think you should stay for the conference," Hugo Victor said as he fixed his tie. "What if the office needs something and I'm unavailable?"

Biting back the sigh on the tip of his tongue, Derek reminded himself that Hugo cared about his business and struggled to hand off the reins to others. "The board is extremely capable and can certainly hold down the fort until you can be reached." Derek handed over the headpiece microphone Hugo would need to wear on stage for his talk.

"True," Hugo muttered, shaking his head as he put the microphone on and waited for Derek to tape it discreetly to his temple. "But what do I do if you're not here and I need something?"

"I don't know, Hugo," Derek said, stopping the impending eye roll at the last minute. "But you're the head of Black Marlin Technologies, so I hope that you can work the problem to find a solution. I've been your right hand for quite a few years. I'm confident you will survive without me for a few days. If an emergency arises and you must return to the office before the end of the conference. You know my number." He tipped Hugo's face to the side. "Have I said how much I don't like how discolored your skin is? You need to see a doctor about this, Hugo."

His boss just waved him away, his opinion about seeing a doctor for his recent unusual symptoms already well known by his assistant. Unfortunately, Derek worried there was a very real problem that he was ignoring. Hugo had been suffering from nausea and skin discoloration for over a month but kept saying it was just stress.

Stress was the very reason why Derek was leaving the convention and heading to his cabin on the lake. Hugo had become increasingly dependent on him to do even the most basic tasks, which put unrelenting stress on his shoulders in a way he hadn't signed up for when he took the job. While he appreciated everything Hugo had done for him over the years, it had become clear to him that he couldn't continue to live this way.

Hired initially as an app designer, Derek had impressed Hugo with his organizational and problem-solving skills. When Hugo's previous assistant left to find greener pastures, he'd asked Derek to take the job. Thinking it could only help him take the next step up the ladder, Derek had jumped at the chance, but it would have been better to look before he leaped. Now, he was essentially holding the hand of a fully grown man who would no longer do basic tasks for himself.

"You'll at least stay for my speech, right?" Hugo asked as though he needed Derek's approval for everything he did.

With a smile on his face to hide his bald-faced lie, he nodded. "Of course. I wouldn't miss it for the world, but I'll leave before you take questions, so don't look for me afterward. I'll already be gone."

"Sure, sure. You deserve a vacation. What's it been now?" he asked, as though Derek was supposed to lie about the fact that it had been over three years, so he did.

"Not so long, but I should check the cabin and prepare it for winter, so the timing worked out great."

"But you'll be back Sunday to drive me to Minneapolis, right?"

"I would never leave you stranded," Derek promised, patting him on the back and herding him closer to where he'd need to be when they announced his name.

"My water bottle!" Hugo exclaimed, and Derek quickly put a finger on his lips.

"Shh." He hushed him. "It's already waiting for you onstage. They're about to announce your name. You've got this. Everyone here is your target audience, so there's no reason to be nervous. They're here for the sole reason of hearing what you have to say. Promote the new app and you'll have them eating out of your hand." Another bald-faced lie, but Hugo was known for his stage fright.

With a gentle pat on his shoulder, Hugo grinned. "You are good at what you do, Derek, but lying to an old man? That's a new low even for you."

"I would do no such thing. Besides, you're not an old man. Some would say you're in the prime of your life." After one last check to ensure Hugo had everything he needed, Derek patted his back. "I'm going to head out and stand in the back of the room. Good luck!" he exclaimed quietly before he exited stage left.

He never stopped at the back of the room, knowing there wasn't a chance his boss would ever see him in a conference room of that size, so cutting out now gave him extra time to get to his favorite place. He hadn't been to his cabin in too long. It had gotten so bad, he'd started paying a local caretaker to watch over it. Now that it was nearing the end of October, it was time to prepare it for winter with the hope that, next year, he would get to see the inside of it more often.

His cabin, just off Minnesota Highway 61 between Duluth and Two Harbors, had been a staple in his life since he was a kid. First, his grandparents had owned it and when they'd passed, it went to his parents. Since his dad passed away and his mom moved to Florida to live with a group of her bridge club friends, she had gifted it to him. It was always his dream to live there year-round, but the infrastructure wasn't there for such an undertaking, especially during the winter months.

The cool air hit him in the face when he stepped out of the convention center, and he inhaled deeply, the fresh air invigorating him. As he pulled off his suit coat and tie in preparation for the short drive along the scenic highway, the gently lapping waves against the shore of Lake Superior reminded him why work couldn't be his entire life. When he pulled onto the highway, he chuckled at the thought. He already knew that, but he was sure Hugo had missed that memo.

Derek had four days to figure out how to break the news to his boss that their time together was coming to a close.

"Please welcome our first presenter. A man who needs no introduction, Mr. Hugo Victor!"

Alayah had to force herself not to roll her eyes as she motioned for Zac to cut the master of ceremony's mic. The dude had spent the first fifteen minutes of the conference giving the audience instructions like a drill sergeant and the next fifteen minutes introducing Hugo as if he were up for an Emmy. Apparently, the man needed plenty of introduction. She reminded herself that she was jaded by the years she had spent in a place full of people who thought their newest tech development made them God's gift to the green earth. The truth was, they weren't any different from the last guy who had been standing up there. While his tenure had been long, in the end, the same could be said for Hugo Victor, but she knew better than to say that around this crowd.

When he walked out onto the stage, the audience stood, giving him a standing ovation before he had so much as uttered a word. That wasn't the reason her gaze tracked around the room. She was pinpointing where the Secure One agents were stationed and taking count. She had Cal on one side and Eric on the other side of the stage, Roman and Mack in the aisle to her left, and Jonah and Lucas on her right. Next to her sat Declan and Zac, whom she had commandeered when she was informed that she would be running all the equipment for the presentations. She couldn't do that alone. Thankfully, it gave Cal plenty of time to get more men to Duluth before the conference officially got underway.

"Good morning, Northland," Hugo said from the stage, and she adjusted his microphone to subtly improve the tone throughout the room.

From there, she handed the AV equipment controls to

Zac and Declan so she could concentrate on keeping the security tight for the convention center's computer programs. Allowing anything to slip past her could open a door for any number of bad players to walk through. Not on her watch. She had every intention of doing her part to keep the conference safe, as that would secure her job for years to come.

She glanced away from her computer to watch Hugo take another drink from his water bottle. He'd been speaking for nearly an hour and had the crowd eating out of the palm of his hand. He walked to the left of the stage and coughed once before he returned to his speech. With her attention focused on the checks and balances of her programs, it took her several moments to realize Hugo had stopped speaking. By the time she looked at the stage, he was crumpling to the ground, gurgling breath sounds filling the auditorium before Zac could cut his mic. Someone screamed before pandemonium ensued. Cal and Roman jumped onstage while the rest of the team moved in to protect the perimeter.

"Call an ambulance," Cal hollered, his fingers to Hugo's neck.

Declan did just that while she turned to Zac. "What just happened?"

"I have no idea, but whatever it is, it's not good."

The tight draw to his lips told her she might have just watched a man die.

Chapter Three

It was close to dark when Derek returned to the cabin after spending a few hours fishing from the dock. He had arrived before noon and spent the afternoon cleaning up around the property and splitting some firewood to use once the sun went down and the night cooled. While he had stopped to pick up groceries, fresh lake trout had sounded like heaven, so he'd grabbed his pole and headed to the shore. He hadn't caught any trout, but the bass and crappies in his basket would taste just as good. All it took was one afternoon on the lake to solidify his decision to leave the city and strike out on his own. The four hours he'd spent away from his phone had been peaceful, but he made a mental note to check it once he got back inside, just in case Hugo had called. There was very little cell coverage out here, but he'd found the left corner of his kitchen counter was the one place the phone had reception.

As he cleaned and filleted the fish, he let his mind wander to the infinite possibilities that life held for him if he got off the hamster wheel, which told him the time had come to walk away. He was working too much but not reaping the benefits of the time spent. Did he have to work? Yes. Did he have to devote every waking minute to making someone else money while he settled for a salary that would never equal his worth? No. Would Hugo Victor understand that? Also no. But he could no longer use that as the reason he didn't stand up for himself.

Ultimately, Hugo himself was the only reason he'd continued in the position for as long as he had. He'd become like a father to him and the last thing Derek wanted to do was hurt him. Unfortunately, he also couldn't continue with the status quo. Once they returned to the city, he'd sit down and have a serious conversation with him. The unhealthy pallor of his boss's skin crossed his mind, and he amended that statement. After Hugo went to the doctor, he'd sit him down and have a conversation with him. Thankfully, Derek had taken it upon himself to make him an appointment for next week. Something just didn't sit right with him about how his boss had been acting lately.

He grabbed the fish and his cleaning supplies and walked into the cabin, pushing the door open with his butt so he could make his way to the sink to wash the fish and his knives. He was drying the fish when he felt a presence behind him. Just a whisper of air that told him he wasn't alone. He grabbed a knife and spun around, barely dodging a fist that glanced off his jaw without doing much damage.

The man before him was dressed head to toe in black and carried a small gun that was likely just as deadly as a big one would be. Derek put up his hands in defense.

"Take whatever you want," he said slowly. "I don't want any trouble."

"Where are the files?" The guy's voice was deep and booming inside the small cabin.

"What files?" Derek asked, having no sooner finished the sentence when that fist darted out again to land a lightning punch on his nose and lip, blood spurting across the floor from one or the other or both. The pain momentarily filled his vision with stars. “I don’t know what files you want, man!” he exclaimed, dodging another blow to his face that landed on his right eye rather than his already sore nose.

“The app,” he grumbled, shoving the gun into Derek’s chest.

Derek wanted to play dumb, but with the gun in such close proximity to his heart, he opted for a lie instead. “The computer bag,” he said, his fat lip making it hard to speak. “Jump drive in the outside pocket.”

“Get it,” the guy said, motioning him toward it with the gun. “Drop the knife, and don’t make any wrong moves. We’ll get the drive, and then we’ll keep walking out the front door. You’re coming with me.”

Derek had forgotten he was holding the knife but dropped it immediately. He then walked slowly toward the front of the cabin, where his computer bag sat on the desk. The room had been ransacked, telling him he’d interrupted the guy’s search when he’d returned from the lake. He noticed the dark SUV in the driveway that he couldn’t see from the kitchen. The lights were off, but he could hear the motor. It had a little tic in its idle that he concentrated on as he walked to the bag and fumbled with it while he searched for an out. The old saying, “Don’t bring a knife to a gunfight,” ran through his mind. He tamped down the burst of laughter threatening since he didn’t even have a knife anymore.

Then it hit him. He did have a knife. His personal protection blade was still in his laptop bag, but he’d only have one chance to pull it and tag the guy before he could get off a shot. He dug through the bag, pretending he couldn’t find the drive until the gun barrel dug into his back.

“It’s here, just give me a second. It’s dark, and everything in the bag is black." His hand finally closed around the handle of the knife. "Found it." He would have smiled, but his lip was too swollen, so he took a deep breath and concentrated on the next few moments of his life.

"Hand it over," the guy growled, moving to the side but keeping the gun on him as he held out his other hand.

"With pleasure," Derek said as he spun and jammed the knife into his cheek, eliciting an ear-piercing yowl from the guy.

Derek turned and ran for the back door, praying that the guy's partner in crime wasn't waiting there to take him out. It was a risk he had to take if he stood a chance of making it out alive. A shot rang out, and he braced himself for the burning pain of a bullet that never came, so he plowed through the back door and kept going into the night until the forest swallowed him up, and then he kept running.

Unfortunately, his options were limited with the lake to his front and the guys to his back. He didn't have his phone or a boat, and it was too risky to be on Lake Superior in the dark anyway. He'd have to run parallel to the highway until he was far enough away from the cabin to find help. He was closer to Duluth than Two Harbors, so he turned to the right and headed along the shoreline, darting back into the trees where the shore turned too rocky. It was slow going and often treacherous as a late fall storm blew in, but he couldn't risk stopping despite how badly his head pounded with every step. He could barely breathe, with his nose swollen on one side and his lip blocking the other. He stopped along the shore and scooped up the cold water, repeatedly holding it to his nose and lip until it numbed the pain. Then he got up and kept going.

Derek wondered who those guys were working for until a thought crossed his mind. Josh Hunt. The name made him pause. He didn't see Josh, the owner of Virtual Scorpion Productions, as someone capable of such violence when he could just create his own app. As Black Marlin Technologies' direct competitor in the app world, Josh had plenty of skills, not to mention several tech designers within his company who could create the same kind of app that Black Marlin had developed. Resorting to violence and kidnapping seemed outside the gate for Josh, or anyone, for that matter. He quickened his steps along the gravel road leading him to the highway. Once there, he could figure out how far outside of the city he was and then decide on his next move.

Thankfully, his cabin was on the scenic portion of Highway 61, which meant far less traffic this time of night. It would be easy to spot his attackers if they started searching for him on the deserted highway. He'd find safety somewhere for a few hours, then he'd have to return to his cabin. He didn't care about his phone, computers, or the cabin itself. He cared about the one item he'd hidden away and had to pray those guys didn't find it. Once he had that jump drive in his hands, he'd call the police, but not until then. Five minutes later, he noticed a bar two hundred yards ahead. All he had to do was cross the highway and approach from the other direction. Traffic was light, but he couldn't risk being exposed for too long if those guys were looking for him. He looked left, then right, and took a deep breath as he darted onto the road. It wasn't until he heard a squeal of brakes that he realized his mistake.

"TECH MOGUL HUGO VICTOR collapsed and died at a conference today in Minnesota—"

Alayah switched the radio off with a sigh. She had lived that scene and didn't need the constant reminder. She was beyond tired but keyed up at the same time. A harsh, derisive laugh fell from her lips. That tended to happen when the one person you were supposed to protect ended up dead. The preliminary tox reports said he was poisoned, but no one who'd witnessed it needed a tox report to tell them that. They'd watched it happen in real time. Hugo took a drink from his bottle, got out a few more words, and fell into a heap. She didn't need a degree in medicine to know that something in the bottle had caused it.

The event coordinators had ultimately decided to postpone the conference until they were sure that the attack was aimed at Hugo and no one else, and the police also wanted to locate Hugo's assistant to question him. Her mind immediately returned to the handsome man she'd met earlier that day. He was tall, lean and dressed to impress in a Hugo Boss suit that made her smile at the play on names. Derek Benjamin pulled off the billionaire CEO look without even trying, and she couldn't help but hope he had nothing to do with this. She'd shaken his hand and exchanged witty conversation the whole while he'd held a bottle filled with ethylene glycol. Otherwise known as antifreeze. Did he know? According to Cal and the team, he was the last person to touch the water bottle, having handed it off to them to put on the stage, which Cal had done right before the conference began.

No one could have messed with the bottle after Secure One took possession. All of that said, Cal couldn't prove it. They had a video feed of the water bottle on the stage, but what happened between the handoff and the start of the conference hadn't been recorded. At least, not according to the convention center. Alayah didn't believe it and planned to comb through their recordings from all angles to find proof that Secure One was not on the hook for this.

What she really wanted to know was why Derek didn't answer his phone. The cops wondered if he thought their calls were spam, so they'd even tried calling him from Hugo's phone, but still got no answer. That was… What did the kids call it these days? A little sus? Yeah, she thought so, too. She had every intention of using one of the Secure Watch computers to conduct a little digital investigation on the dude as soon as she arrived back at the hotel. Once they were told the conference was over for the day, she volunteered to meet a team member in Two Harbors who had some extra equipment they needed to sort out this mess with their reputation intact. That included scouring all available camera footage for her team's movements during the morning. Since she couldn't help them with much physically, the least she could do was drive an hour up the road for the handoff.

Exhaustion had crept in the last few miles, though, and she couldn't wait to take a shower and cozy up in bed. She chuckled into the quiet of the car. Like that was going to happen anytime soon. It was all-hands-on-deck, so she still had several hours of work ahead of her when she returned to the hotel. At least Cal promised her a burger and fries when she returned. A yawn escaped just as she caught the tail end of something in her headlight beam. She slammed on the brakes, but it was too late. Whatever she'd hit went flying into the ditch with a scream.

A very human scream.

Chapter Four

Alayah yanked the wheel to the side of the road. She had to radio for help. Getting out of the car was dangerous for her, not to mention there was no way she could walk down the steep ditch in the dark. She'd call 9-1-1 and wait for emergency crews to arrive. Guilt lanced her. What if the person she hit was badly hurt and waiting meant the difference between life and death? Did she have a choice? What could she do to help someone who was gravely injured? Especially if she got injured herself. Before she could make the call, there was a tapping on her window.

A scream ripped from her throat when she turned her head and saw a distorted and bloody face staring at her. Fumbling for the buttons on the phone, the man frantically waved his hand at his neck. That was when it hit her. The man in her window was Derek Benjamin. She put the window down a fraction of an inch.

"Alayah!" he said, his voice breathy and panicked. "You have to help me."

"I was just calling 9-1-1. What were you doing on the road? I can't believe I did that much damage to your face!"

"You didn't," he said quickly, which stopped her hand midair. "You didn't even hit me. I probably have road rash from diving for the ditch, but your fender just missed me.

This—" he motioned at his face with his hand "—is the result of a beating at my cabin. I got jumped about thirty minutes ago. I was heading to that bar to get help when you came around that curve. I didn't even see you coming."

"Probably because one eye is swollen shut," she said, taking stock of the man who was clearly terrified and victimized. "Let me call 9-1-1. You need medical care."

"No time for that," he said, glancing around the deserted road. "Those guys are probably looking for me. We need to get off this road before they see us."

She didn't know Derek Benjamin, but she knew he needed help. She could get him back to Duluth quickly, but could she risk letting him into her vehicle if he'd been responsible for Hugo's death? If what he said was true, and someone was after him, could she live with herself if they found him and killed him? Were they the people behind Hugo's death? It couldn't be a coincidence that Hugo's assistant had been attacked the same day Hugo was killed, right? She didn't have answers to any of these questions except one. She couldn't live with herself if she didn't get him medical attention. She hit the unlock button on the door and motioned to the back seat.

"Get in and stay low," she said. "The dome light is already disabled." While she waited for him to climb in, she pulled out the first-aid kit. Once he was in, she held it out for him to grab. "There's antiseptic and an ice pack in there. Gauze, if your nose is bleeding. Cal will kill me if you get blood all over these leather seats."

She registered his choked laughter as she pulled back onto the road, but her mind was racing. Was she in a car with a killer right now? She had to let Cal or Mina know what was going on without tipping him off. If she pushed her SOS button, they'd know she was in trouble and come looking for her, but something stopped her. Maybe it was the fact that someone had clearly beaten Derek, and the terror she saw in his eyes wasn't something someone could fake.

"I need to find somewhere to turn around. It could take a few minutes."

"Where were you headed?" he asked as she heard the snap of an ice pack. He moaned a little, and she had to assume he was holding the ice pack to his face.

"Two Harbors," she answered. "I'm meeting a colleague to pick up some equipment needed for the conference." Alayah decided to leave out the part where his boss was dead. She wanted to see his reaction when she told him the news. Would she see shock? Surprise? Or something more sinister?

"We're almost to Knife River." he said, but she struggled to understand him with his fat lip, so she focused on him rather than her own unrelenting questions. "Keep going to Two Harbors. Be on the lookout for a black Chevy Tahoe. Every window is tinted."

Alayah fought hard against rolling her eyes so she could keep them on the road. Half the vehicles these days are black SUVs. "If I drive to Two Harbors, it's another forty-five minutes back to Duluth before you can get medical care," she said with a shake of her head. "Though, Two Harbors does have a hospital."

"I don't need medical care," he insisted. "What I need is to get the jump drive with Hugo's new app. I had to ditch the cabin before I could grab it. He'll go ballistic if someone gets their hands on that app. The jump drive is well hidden, but I can't risk leaving the cabin empty for very long."

Hugo would never go ballistic again, but she couldn't tell him that yet, as his statement suggested he didn't know his boss was dead. "Your face says something else entirely." She said instead as they plowed through the darkness. She searched for a cross street, but they were few and far between.

"My nose isn't broken, just swollen. Same with my eye and lip. The ice will help. I can't go anywhere until I go back to my cabin."

"I thought you said that's where you were jumped," she said suspiciously.

"It was. It's also where all my stuff is, including my car, phone and computers. I have to hope the guys cleared out, so I can sneak back in and grab everything. I barely escaped a trip in the back of an SUV to an unknown place. I didn't have time to pack."

"Wait, they tried to kidnap you?"

"You betcha," he agreed, to which she smiled. Leave it to a Minnesotan to answer such a serious question with "You betcha."

"Why?"

"That's what I'd like to know as well," he answered. "I have no idea who they were or why they were there, other than they wanted the files to an app."

"Like a work app?"

"That was my vibe. I convinced him it was in my bag, where I had my defense blade. I stabbed him with it while he was distracted and then took off running. He took a shot at me but missed, so I kept going without looking back."

"Hardcore," she muttered, trying to decide if she bought his story. It could just as easily be that he'd instigated the fight and someone escaped from him. The scenario didn't sit right with her, though. None of this sat right with her, and she had no idea what to do. What would Cal do? Cal would have called 9-1-1 rather than let the guy into his car. A glance in the rearview mirror said that ship sailed.

"If only I knew who they were and what they wanted," he muttered from the back seat. "I suspect it has something to do with a new app from work."

Her ears perked up as she drove. "Do you think it's the app that Hugo was promoting today?"

"No way to know for sure," he hedged. "We have a lot of apps."

"But?" she asked. "I'm sensing a but."

"There are a lot of unsaid buts there. I'm trying to sort it all out, but my nose is making my head pound. Thankfully, the ice is helping."

"There should be pain-relief powder in the kit," she said. "I'd hand you water, but I use hand controls and can't take them off the wheel."

Before she finished, she heard the rip of paper, telling her he'd found the powder. "Bless you," he said, and she could see him downing the powder in her rearview mirror. "I can't thank you enough for the ride. Tell me you wouldn't give just any bloodied stranger on the side of the road a ride. That's not safe."

"It's fair to say you're the first and, once Cal hears about this, the last bloodied stranger I'll pick up off the side of the road. That said, I'm a good judge of character and you didn't do that to your own face."

"Never. This face is too pretty to scuff up."

She laughed, then the SUV fell silent. She didn't know what he was thinking; but chances were good it wasn't the same thing she was thinking. He was right about picking up random strangers off the road. Cal was going to have words for her, but she stood by her decision. Derek wasn't dangerous, but someone certainly had it out for him. "We're hitting the city limits of Two Harbors," she said. "I'm supposed to meet my colleague at McDonald's to transfer the equipment. He'll have to do it since I can't reach the back of this SUV. Explaining why you're in the back seat is going to take some time." She rolled her eyes at herself. That was an understatement since she could be harboring a fugitive in a company-owned car.

"There's a gas station coming up on the right," he said, gathering the first-aid kit. "Drop me there. I'll hide in the bathroom and clean myself up. When you're done, swing back and grab me."

"What if those guys show up?" she asked, unable to keep the skepticism from her voice.

"If you see a black Chevy Tahoe in the parking lot, keep going," he said. "Otherwise, it should be fine for the few minutes you'll be gone. I still have my wallet, so I'll grab some water and be on the lookout for you. How long will it take to grab the equipment?"

"Fifteen minutes tops. Kieran knows I need to return to Duluth quickly." When the gas station came into view, she signaled right and turned in, pulling off to the side of the building that was shrouded in darkness. "What if I don't return?" she asked as he cracked the door.

"I'd understand and wish you all the best in life, Alayah. Thanks for helping me get this far. I don't know who those guys are or what they want, but at least you gave me a fighting chance to stay alive long enough to find out. The only way to do that is to return to my cabin."

Before she could say another word, he carefully closed the door behind him and disappeared into the darkness.

THE DARK HELPED hide his busted-up face, but Derek knew walking into the store would make it harder to cover. He was grateful he'd still been wearing his ball cap when he got jumped. At least he could keep his head down, but just in case, he already had a lie on the tip of his tongue. As long as the store clerk didn't decide to call the cops, he'd be fine.

He waited for Alayah to back out and disappear before he walked toward the store. What were the chances that the one person he'd run across on a dark highway would be her? He didn't think the odds were high, yet it had happened, and he'd been grateful the face staring back at him had been friendly. He noticed the clerk turn and walk toward the back of the store, so he slid through the door and headed toward the sign that read Restrooms. He was grateful the door locked, preventing anyone from walking in on him. He set the first-aid kit down on the sink and took stock of his face. It was bad, but not as bad as he expected. The ice pack must have slowed the swelling because he could almost see out of his eye again. He used paper towels and warm water to clean the blood off his face and lip. Once the blood was gone, he could tell his nose wasn't broken. It was swollen and tender, but another hour of ice should take care of that. He'd get a bag from the vending machine to use on the way back to the cabin once Alayah picked him up.

If she picked him up.

He wouldn't blame her if she kept driving straight out of town. There was no reason to get herself or her employer mixed up in whatever this was. Sure, she worked for a security firm, but that didn't mean they wanted the kind of trouble he was facing, whatever that trouble might be. If she didn't return in thirty minutes, he'd get a room at the hotel in town and call Hugo. He should be warned that someone was after company files, and hopefully, he'd send someone out to pick him up.

A hint of a smile cracked his lips when he thought about

how he'd much rather ride back to Duluth with Alayah than Hugo. She was sharp, assessing and intelligent, as evidenced by their conversation in the car. She was beautiful, though he suspected she'd downplay the compliment should he offer it. While she was sharp, assessing, and intelligent, she didn't seem to have a lot of self-confidence. He could tell by the way she'd hesitated when talking to him in the car. Then again, maybe she was hesitant because she had just picked up a man she didn't know, who looked like he had gone ten rounds in the ring. *Assuming anything else makes you an ass, Derek Benjamin*, and that was the last thing he wanted to be when it came to Alayah Heath. She intrigued him, but unfortunately for him, their paths had likely crossed at the wrong time in life and he would never get the chance to know her better.

After repacking the first-aid kit and dumping his garbage, he checked his watch. She'd been gone five minutes, so he had ten more minutes to kill before deciding what to do for the evening. He longed for a soft pillow and more pain meds, but that would have to wait. What he really needed was to get back to his cabin and see what was left for him to grab. He sent up a silent prayer his attackers hadn't burned the place down just to spite him. The jump drive with the app on it wasn't the only one, but he didn't want it to fall into the wrong hands either. He had to get it before he did anything else.

He headed for the fountain machine and filled a bag with ice, holding it to his nose and lip for a fast shot of relief. The television in the corner drew his eye and he squinted to read the headline on the screen: Hugo Victor Dies at Local Convention Center. More at 10:00.

Derek blinked twice as he walked closer to the television. The time in the corner said 9:59, so he stood transfixed until the newscaster came on to report the breaking news. Since the volume was low, he had to read the subtitles.

Hugo Victor, age 62, collapsed and died during a tech talk at a local convention center in Duluth. Authorities report the investigation into his death is ongoing.

Derek took a step back as they segued into the life and times of Hugo Victor. His boss was *dead*? Why hadn't anyone called him? Why hadn't Alayah said anything? Maybe she'd thought he already knew? He pictured his phone, which he'd left plugged into a charger at the cabin. Coverage was spotty in that area, so he never bothered to take it with him when he was on the property. Since he'd been jumped immediately upon his return, he'd never checked it for messages. Had Curtis or one of the other board members tried to reach him? They had full control of the business whenever Hugo was on the road, but surely, he would have reached out to let Derek know what had happened. Or had he thought Derek had still been there and was already aware of his boss's death, thus wondering why he hadn't called the office?

A shot of fear filled him at the thought that maybe the beating at his cabin was tied to Hugo's death. Then again, they didn't say his death was suspicious, so maybe it was just a coincidence? Derek grabbed two bottles of water from the cooler and a bottle of ibuprofen while on autopilot. Hugo was dead. His heart seized in his chest and he forced the engulfing emotions back. He didn't have the luxury of falling apart in a gas station in the middle of nowhere when someone was after him. He had to keep his wits about him in case the beating at his cabin was tied to Hugo's death. They didn't say how Hugo died, so it might not be connected, but even his concussed brain didn't believe that. It was connected, and it was his job to figure out how before those guys found him again.

Paying the cashier, who didn't appear to care that he looked like he'd been in a bar brawl, he noticed the time on the wall clock. Alayah would be back for him any minute—if she returned for him. Something deep inside him said she would because, whether she believed it or not, she was his hero and wouldn't leave him stranded. She already had one opportunity to do that, but followed her gut instead. When he left the safety of the station to stand in the shadows, he knew she'd do it again.

Thinking back over the events of the night, he hoped his beating and Hugo's death were an unfortunate coincidence. If they weren't, he was in far more danger than he'd thought just five minutes ago.

Chapter Five

Alayah had apologized profusely to Kieran for being late. It hadn't been by much, but she lied that she'd run into some problems on the road. He was new to Secure Watch, and she didn't want him to think she was wasting his time. He assured her she was fine as he'd run into some problems on the road with wildlife too. She was okay with letting him think the problems she encountered on the road were from wildlife. Telling him she was driving around with a possible murder suspect in the back of her SUV would have gotten her a ticket to Cal's office without passing go.

Now she was at a crossroads. Did she swing back through the gas station and get Derek, or did she continue driving? The smart answer was to continue driving and pretend she'd never met Derek Benjamin. The problem was that she couldn't live with herself if Derek was innocent and he got hurt or killed because she was too afraid to help him. She decided to pick him up and drive him to his cabin. From there, he was on his own. Once he was out of her car, she'd make sure to tell him the cops wanted to question him about his boss's death. No sense opening herself up to a hostage situation. Not that she could get there with the handsome stranger. By all accounts, he was kind, funny and probably a saint to put up with Hugo Victor for a boss. But people often said some of those things about serial killers, too.

Her giggle filled the car. If Derek had laced his boss's water with antifreeze, he probably wouldn't have stuck around to see if it worked. As she pulled into the station, Derek emerged from the shadows. Staying low, he slid into the back seat and closed the door. When she glanced up into the rearview mirror, she noticed the look on his face.

"Why didn't you tell me Hugo is dead?"

She bit her lip as she tried to think of a workable lie. "I thought you knew."

"You thought I knew and just didn't bring it up in the twenty minutes we were on the road?"

Rather than speak, she put the car into Reverse and backed out, turning onto the highway. "It seemed like you had bigger fish to fry."

"How did he die?" he asked, the words desperate to her ears.

"You don't know?"

"No, how would I know?" he asked, shifting on the seat. "The report on the television said he collapsed and died, and authorities are investigating. Was it a heart attack? He did have high cholesterol and high blood pressure. He was also high-strung."

"I don't think his high cholesterol had anything to do with being poisoned."

There was silence from the back seat. "Did you say poisoned?"

"I did," she answered. "With antifreeze."

"Alayah, my boss, who was also my friend, just died. It's cruel to be sarcastic at a time like this."

She shook her head as she peered through the murky

darkness. "Trust me when I say there's no sarcasm detected in that statement. I was there and watched it happen."

"You watched it happen?"

"Yep," she said, swallowing down the bile. "He took a drink from his bottle and said a few more words before he collapsed."

The silence from the back seat was deafening.

"Derek?"

He leaned over the seat, making her jump, but she bit back the shriek that had tried to escape. "You're saying the antifreeze was in the water bottle?"

"That's the assumption," she said. "That's need-to-know information, by the way. I only know because the water bottle was in our care for a period of time."

Alayah knew the moment the realization hit him. He threw himself backward in the seat as though he'd been punched. "They think I did it!"

"They certainly want to talk to you," she agreed. "The cops are looking for you as we speak. I'm surprised law enforcement didn't show up at your cabin already."

"No one knows where it is," he answered, his hand on his forehead. When she didn't say anything, he sighed. "That was on purpose. If Hugo knew where to find me on the rare occasion I left the city, he wouldn't hesitate to bombard me with never-ending tasks. The cops will eventually find the location, but the deed is in my mom's name, so it will probably take them some time. Doesn't matter. Once we stop at the cabin and pick up my things, you can drop me off at the station. I have nothing to hide."

Alayah was silent as they drove, allowing him a few moments to think about what she'd told him. She didn't know him well, but she was sure that he hadn't faked surprise at the news that his boss was poisoned. He didn't know what was going on, and the wild look in his eye told her he was either scared or concussed. Then again, it was probably both.

"How did the antifreeze get in the water bottle?" he asked, as though the thought just struck him. "I poured his special vitamin water out of the original bottle and into his and then handed it to Cal."

"You dumped already bottled water into another bottle?"

He nodded with exaggeration. "Ridiculous, I know. Hugo was superstitious. He always insisted that the water bottle had to be with him at every event for it to be successful."

"Man," she muttered. "That would be a serious problem if you ever lost it."

His laughter was surprising in the face of the conversation, but even she could admit that he was probably still in shock. "We had four of those same bottles, Alayah. He never knew that, but there was no way I was getting caught unable to find one."

"Wait, so there are other bottles?"

"Yes, but I left the extras at home since I wouldn't be with Hugo. I cautioned him that he had to keep an eye on it because if he lost it, I couldn't help him."

"Sounds like you treated him like a child," she observed, glancing in the rearview mirror. He was incredibly handsome, even with a bruised eye, nose and lip. She was glad to see that the swelling had subsided, now allowing him to open it fully.

"Everyone knew who Hugo Victor was," he said with a shrug. "He liked being catered to, and despite owning and running a multibillion-dollar company, he also wanted people to hold his hand when it came to just about everything else."

"Some people would call that eccentric," she said, to which he shrugged.

"Others call it self-indulgent and lazy. I call it exhausting. You need to turn soon to get to my cabin. It's just on the other side of Knife River."

She was silent for a moment, wondering why on earth he thought it was smart to go back to his cabin when he'd been attacked there just hours before. "Maybe it's a better idea to just go to Duluth. What if those guys are waiting?"

"It's a chance I have to take," he said, and then let silence prevail.

HUGO HAD BEEN poisoned with antifreeze via his water bottle. Derek still couldn't wrap his mind around that. What was worse was that they thought he had something to do with it. He had literally no idea it was ever used that way other than on television or in detective novels.

"Does antifreeze kill someone that quickly?" His question was aloud, but he hadn't intended for her to answer.

"According to our sources, as little as four ounces of it can kill a man. He'd been sipping at the bottle for at least an hour before he collapsed, and it was over half empty by report."

"The bottle holds twenty ounces."

"It wasn't straight antifreeze, though. He would have known if that was the case. It was mixed with something else. The police suspect the chemical caused a heart attack. Now that you've mentioned his other heart conditions, that seems more likely."

"I still can't believe it." A shudder went through him at the thought of poor Hugo drinking antifreeze. The saddest thing was that Hugo died with few to mourn him. Sure, he had friends, but true family was nonexistent. Due to his work, he never married, and his desire to become one of the world's richest tech gurus drove a wedge between him and his extended family.

Derek always wondered if that was one of the reasons why Hugo depended on him so much. He didn't need Derek to do everything for him. He just needed to feel close to someone. Hugo saw Derek as much as a son as an employee. They'd worked together for years, planning and creating apps. Derek moaned. If only he'd talked to Hugo sooner about how he was feeling.

"Are you okay?" Alayah asked as she slowed for the gravel road near his cabin.

"Fine," he lied, sitting forward again. "Let's drive past the cabin slowly. It sits to the front of the lot, so we'll know if anyone is in the driveway besides my sedan."

"I hope there's an outlet somewhere because I can't turn around easily on this narrow road."

He nodded and pointed straight ahead. "If we see anyone else parked there, floor it to the end of the road. You can turn back onto the highway there."

"I'm driving, you're checking," she said, eyes straight ahead.

Derek could hear the fear in her voice, but he didn't say anything. She was trying to help him, and while he could go to Duluth, explain the situation to the police, and then try to convince them to take him to the cabin, there was no guarantee they would. He needed the information sooner rather than later if he was going to prove his innocence or, at the very least, give them reasonable doubt.

"You're doing fine," he assured her, patting her shoulder. "I'm aware that I'm asking a lot from someone you just met, and I wouldn't blame you if you just keep driving, but

I implore you not to. If we're going to find Hugo's killer quickly, the information inside that cabin is imperative."

"Those guys, though," she said, and he shook his head.

"Those guys are long gone. Once I bolted, I'm sure they just grabbed my bags and took off. I'd already told him what he was looking for was in my bag, and they couldn't be sure I wouldn't call the cops. I would guess they wouldn't want to be there if I did."

"That's fair, but maybe we should call Cal. He could send some guys out to cover you while you go in."

Derek couldn't argue that it was a bad idea. It just wasn't a timely one. For every minute he waited to present to the police, he looked more and more guilty. They might even think he hid the cabin's address to keep them from finding him. Why would he stick around town if he'd poisoned his boss, though? That didn't make any sense and was the exact question he would pose to them when he finally arrived in the city.

"I would understand if that made you more comfortable, but do you want to get your employer involved in this?"

The car jerked slightly as it came to a stop. "Secure Inc. is already up to its ears in this, Derek. The equipment in the hatch is meant to help us track down Hugo's killer faster and more effectively than sitting in the dark by a cabin that's already been broken into once. I should be back in Duluth doing my job, but I'm here with you instead. We've never been more involved in this. Besides, Cal has been involved in cases with much higher stakes than a dead billionaire tech mogul."

Derek couldn't deny that. Secure Inc. had been involved in some high-profile cases, with the implications of the most recent Secure Watch cases traveling through the tech industry like a ripple. From a Trojan horse that took control of video cameras around the world to a hostage situation in a biohazard lab, they'd had their fair share of notoriety when it came to being involved in, and ultimately solving cases like this. Having Secure Watch on his side could only help him, so getting one of their operatives messed up in this probably wasn't the smartest move. He just wished he had a choice.

"That's fair, but it's also a lot of time wasted. Let's just drive by and see what we see. If all is quiet, I can be in and out in a matter of minutes."

Alayah let off the brake with a sigh, and the SUV rolled forward at a crawl. As they passed the cabin, he noticed a single light glowed from the back. It revealed his sedan in the driveway, but no other vehicles. She pressed down slowly on the accelerator as she drove down the gravel road.

"There's a light on in there," she said, approaching the stop sign at the end of the road.

"It's in the kitchen. I turned it on right before that guy jumped me," he explained. "I'm not surprised they didn't shut it off before they left. I wouldn't be surprised if both doors were hanging open, too. There weren't any cars in the driveway, so it's safe to return."

"Ha," she said as they came to the stop sign. "For all you know, one of them is lying in wait for you."

"Doubtful," he said with a shake of his head. "They got what they wanted from me."

"They think they did, but when they figure out you lied to them, they'll be back," she said, her voice filled with nerves.

No one could say she wasn't smart. The fact was, he had no choice, but he didn't have to drag her with him.

"Let me out," he said, patting her shoulder. "I'll go by myself, get what I need, and hightail it back here. I could drive into town, but they know my car now. That's a risk I can't take this late at night with so few cars on the road."

Alayah opened her mouth to speak just as ringing filled the car's interior. Both their gazes darted to the console, where Cal's name was flashing on the screen. With a grimace, she reached out and punched the button. It felt like a punch to his gut, but he couldn't blame her. He'd have done the same thing.

Chapter Six

Alayah's heart was pounding. Everything was happening so quickly she couldn't wrap her head around any of it. Not for the first time in her life, she wished she was braver and wasn't afraid of the things the guys at Secure One faced daily without fear. Or at least, that's what it seemed like to her. Maybe, just this once, she could be brave. The ringing stopped, and she swore she heard Derek let out a relieved sigh from the back.

"He probably checked the GPS and noticed I was stopped," she explained.

"You should have answered," Derek said as she put the SUV in Reverse and turned it back down the gravel road. It was no easy task, but Cal would start to worry if she didn't get the vehicle moving.

"He'll call back, and I'll have to answer," she said, pulling into the cabin's driveway. "You have two minutes to get what you need or I'm out," she said through gritted teeth. He grasped the door handle when something occurred to her. "Wait." She put the vehicle in Park and opened the console, coming up with a gun. "Take this. Just in case. It's loaded. No safety. Point and shoot."

"You're giving a possible murderer a gun?" he asked,

accepting it carefully before he grabbed the door handle again.

"If I had any serious concerns that you were a murderer, I wouldn't have picked you up in the first place," she answered. "Don't make me regret this."

"As the kids say, BRB." Then he was gone, his shadow stealthy as he slid along the side of the cabin.

She noticed it was less a cabin and more a log home, which was probably gorgeous in the daylight. Tonight, though, it was ominous. It was a good reminder that she was a cybersecurity tech, not a security guy. She was about as effective in an emergency as a mouse, and fear mixed with the acid in her stomach as she watched Derek peek in several of the windows on his way past them. He must be headed for the back door to make sure no one was waiting for him there. She braced herself for the retort of the gun but heard none. Before long, the light went out in the kitchen, and she held her breath, hoping he'd been the one to turn it off. The phone rang again, and she jumped at the sudden intrusion to her thoughts. On instinct she hit the button to answer.

"Secure Watch, Alpha," she said, using their greeting code. If anyone ever answered without using the greeting, the caller knew there was a problem and would send help. She always thought her code name was hilarious. There was no one less alpha than her, but maybe tonight was her chance to be one.

"Secure One, Charlie. Alayah? Are you okay?" Cal asked, concern lacing his words. "You should be back by now, but when I checked the GPS, you weren't moving."

"Sorry for the holdup," she said, as though she couldn't prevent it when she very well could. "I got turned around when I took a side road to avoid hitting a deer. 'Tis the season in Minnesota. You know how October is on the roads."

"Especially out there," he agreed. "Do you need an assist?"

"Nope, I'm headed back to the highway as soon as we hang up. Gotta use the hand controls."

"Call me if you need help. Otherwise, I'll see you in twenty."

"You got it, boss," she answered.

"Charlie out," he said, and the line went dead.

She hated lying to Cal, and she'd make sure to apologize when she got back to Duluth. If Lady Luck was on her side, their little adventure tonight would help solve the case they were partially on the hook for, at least the way it stood now. If the jump drive Derek was trying to retrieve could clear him, then it would be that much easier for her to clear Cal. She had to admit the idea of an unknown murderer got her investigative juices going. She yearned to put her hands on a keyboard and dig deep into Hugo Victor's life.

"Just because Derek hasn't hurt you, doesn't mean he didn't hurt Hugo," she muttered to the empty car. "But apparently, you've already decided he's innocent. Is that because you don't think he's capable of murder or is it because his handsome face, great sense of humor and kindness have lulled you into a sense of safety?"

If she were honest with herself, it was mostly the latter. She didn't know him well enough to say with all certainty that he hadn't planned the murder of his boss. But if she listened to her gut, which she'd done since she was old enough to understand how to, Derek wasn't a threat. It was far more likely that he was being threatened, and if she didn't get them back to Duluth soon, the guys who beat him might return.

Movement caught her eye and she glanced up to see Derek hoofing it back to the SUV. She hit the unlock button, and he dove in, slamming the door behind him. Alayah was backing out of the driveway before he was even upright.

"Did you find it?"

"Yes," he said, his voice breathy. "All was quiet, but as I suspected, they had taken my computer bags. Unfortunately, my car key was in one of them."

"You didn't want to drive the car anyway," she reminded him.

"Not until they catch whoever those guys are," he agreed. "Now that they know my car, it will remain in the driveway. Sure, the dealer could cut me a key, but I'd rather not be caught dead in it right now."

"Which is what you might be if you drive it," she said grimly. "They'll be back once they discover you lied to them about what they wanted."

"It'll be too late," he said, holding up a can of soup and shaking it.

"Soup? You're going to fix this situation with chicken noodle soup?" she asked incredulously.

"Nope," he answered, popping off the bottom and holding up a black jump drive. "I'm going to do it with this."

"That's what they were after?" she asked as she slowed for the stop sign.

"Well, the files on it, but yes," he said, throwing it up and catching it in his fist. "Most of the coding for Hugo's new cybersecurity app is on this drive. I say most, because we aren't dumb enough to put the entire program on one drive."

"Ever think about keeping it in a cloud? Feels less dangerous than where we are at the moment," she said, tongue in cheek.

"Clouds can be hacked, according to Hugo. In fact, this program is designed to make a cloud a fortress. It has all the typical features of a cybersecurity app, such as malware protection, threat detection, firewall management and network monitoring. It also has built-in antivirus software, endpoint detection and response tools. The coup de grace is, once it's finished, it can bypass a VPN and detect the actual IP address of the user."

Alayah's breath caught in her chest. "If that's true, Derek, it changes the entire landscape of the digital world and cybersecurity."

"Trust me, it's true," he said, leaning back in the seat as she stopped at the stop sign. "I can't deny Hugo was a genius at what he did."

She could hear the genuine sadness in his words. She didn't believe for a second that he'd killed his boss, but someone had, and doing it with poison made it a personal vendetta. At least in her opinion. Why wait until he was in a room full of people to do it? Showmanship? To make a point? Then it hit her.

To frame Derek.

"Granted," he continued, "there were a lot of people who worked on this project, but in the end, Hugo's brilliance got us this far."

"But why kill Hugo for an app that isn't complete yet? If they do get their hands on it, can they complete the code without Hugo?"

"No," he answered slowly as he leaned forward. "While this app has had multiple coders working on it, Hugo was the only one who could finish it. He would code the bypassing of the VPN aspect of the app, as he was the one who figured out a way around it. At least he thought he had."

"Hmm." Alayah sat at the stop sign, thinking. She was confused about why someone would kill the only person who could turn an ordinary cybersecurity app into a groundbreaking one. "If that's the case, Derek, it leads me to think someone didn't want that app to see the light of day. Did people know that he was the only one who could code it?"

"That wasn't public knowledge. A handful of people knew, at most. I also know where he's stored the coding for the VPN workaround, but no one else does."

"There's your motive. If you killed him, you could swoop in and use his code to finish the app."

"Alayah, I swear on my mother's life that I didn't kill Hugo. He was both my boss and my friend. The real killer wants the police to assume I did it because I'm the easy answer. If they pin it on me, they won't dig any deeper. I must admit, the setup was on point—" The words froze on his lips when a black SUV blocked the intersection, and another pinned them in from behind.

Derek dropped a curse word that told her how much trouble they were in. "They want me. Don't get out of the vehicle," he said as guys approached both sides of her SUV, guns pointed at their heads. She had seconds to decide what to do. She could try to ram the Suburban blocking them in, but her car was smaller and would never push it out of the way. The ditch on both sides was too deep to go down and back up onto the road. Trying to drive in Reverse might work, but she could also land them in the ditch if she wasn't careful.

"Unlock the doors!" one of the guys shouted.

"Do it, but don't get out," he said, far more calmly than she felt, so she reached for the button.

"Do you still have the gun?"

"Yes," he answered. "But it won't do me any good when it's four against one. I'll go with them. You report it to the police."

"Ha," she said, her heart pounding hard against her ribs.

"If you think for a hot second that they aren't going to take me, too, you're delusional."

She calculated the distance from here to Duluth and knew there was no way to stall these guys long enough for Cal to send help. After she hit the unlock button, she pressed a button hidden under her shirt. Her panic button was now their only hope.

Chapter Seven

The two burliest dudes pulled their doors open and dragged them out of the car. Alayah yelped when he dropped her to the ground, fear lancing through her when her ankle sent a jolt of pain up her leg. She was dead if she couldn't run.

"Be careful!" Derek yelled at one of them. "You could hurt her!"

If she hadn't been so terrified, she might have smiled at his protectiveness, but there was nothing to smile about when there was a gun pointed at her face. Besides, she doubted that these guys cared who they hurt.

"She has nothing to do with this," Derek went on. "I'm the one you want. Just let her go."

"Not happening," the guy with the gun growled. "You're both coming with us."

He reached for her, but she scrambled away, afraid if he grabbed her arm, he might break it, rendering her useless in helping Derek. "I'll get up!" she yelled, pushing herself to standing. She wanted to inch closer to Derek, but too many guns were trained at her.

"Toss the gun," the guy holding one on Derek said. "And don't make any sudden moves. You're surrounded, so I promise you, you'll both be dead if you do."

"Feel free to take it," Derek said, turning his back to the guy holding him at gunpoint. "We're all friends here."

Alayah grimaced when the guy took the gun from the waistband of Derek's pants and then shoved him from behind. He went flying and sprawled out in the gravel beside her. He popped back up almost immediately and brushed off his hands.

"We're not friends," the guy snarled. "You wouldn't have lied to a friend about where the information was that he wanted."

"I didn't lie," Derek said, posturing until he managed to block her with his body. "I told you where the files were."

Alayah noticed one of the men touch the giant bandage on his face and she got a little satisfaction knowing he was the one Derek had stabbed. The bandage had blood seeping through it, and he probably needed a hospital, but they were too determined to finish the job. Since they were standing just off a populated highway, even if it was dark, they took the risk of someone seeing them. The thought hit her in the gut. They weren't worried about collateral damage, and that terrified her.

As though one guy read her thoughts, he opened the back hatch of the Suburban. "We can't stand here all night. Get in."

The guys herded them toward the back of the SUV. Alayah limped toward it but knew getting in meant certain death. What choice did she have? Four guys with guns trumped two people without them. Especially when one was nothing more than an ankle-biter in a fight. When they reached the back of the SUV, Derek held his hands up.

"She can't get in herself. I'm going to lift her. I'm not trying anything."

"Boss," one of the other guys said. "We ain't gotta kidnap them. We just gotta get the files. Ain't nobody said nothing about kidnapping no one."

Those few sentences told Alayah that these guys were flying by the seat of their pants rather than following a set plan.

"Ain't nobody asked for your opinion," the boss said, turning away from them to argue with the other guy.

"Can you run?" Derek whisper-asked and she glanced up to meet his gaze. His eyes told her he'd try anything to save them, and she suspected hers reflected the same level of desperation.

"Not on this terrain or with my ankle throbbing the way it is," she whispered as the guys behind them started to argue among themselves.

They listened, hoping for some piece of information they could use once they got out of the situation. Alayah refused to believe that they wouldn't, because if she gave up fighting, she'd be dead.

"We don't have time for this!" the boss yelled, and all the other guys stopped talking, which made it easier for them to hear. "Our job is to get the information. Once we do that, we're out of here. Now shut up, get back in your car, and let's get out of here."

In the second of silence that followed, a twig snapped. "What was that?" the boss asked as they all turned to the woods.

"Probably an animal. I think there are wolves and bears around here," one of them said, and Alayah heard the skitter in his voice.

Something told her it wasn't a wolf or a bear. She glanced up at Derek. *Put me in the car*, she mouthed. Without question, he lifted her carefully by the hips up and into the back of the SUV before she motioned him in. He lowered the hatch while the guys were facing the woods, looking for a threat on four legs. Alayah suspected they'd be surprised to discover the animals they were about to meet only used two.

"What's going on?" Derek asked.

"Do you still have the jump drive?"

He shook his head. "No, I shoved it down in the seats of your SUV. No way will I hand that over willingly to these guys. I'd run while they are distracted, but I'm afraid we'd end up with bullets in our backs."

"Running won't be necessary," she said with a smirk just as the first grunt of pain hit their ears.

"Secure One, Romeo," a voice called out, and Alayah did an internal fist pump.

"Secure Watch, Alpha!" she called when Derek pushed the hatch open. She threw herself at Roman, who caught her, lifting her from the car and setting her down on the road. "I'm so happy to see you!"

Derek climbed out behind her and looked around in confusion. "How?" he asked, taking in the four guys already zip-tied on the ground. Zac and Declan stood with their hands on their hips and frowns on their faces as they stared her down.

"Everyone, this is—"

"Derek Benjamin," Roman finished, but didn't take Derek's outstretched hand. "We've been looking for you. I will say I'm a bit surprised to find you with one of our technicians." He turned to her. "Is this your deer?"

Shame filled her and she willed her body to be still, but she was shaking too much from relief. "I promise I'll explain everything, but we need to get out of here," she said. "How did you get here so quickly?"

"We managed to track down Derek's cabin earlier tonight," Roman explained.

"That was fast," Derek said, obviously shocked.

"The head of Secure Watch, my wife," Roman added, "worked for the FBI. Finding your cabin was child's play for someone like Mina."

Alayah heard so much pride in Roman's voice whenever he spoke of Mina. She dreamed about hearing that come from a man who loved her, but she knew that was a long shot at best. She might be little, but she was a lot to love for so many reasons. Thus far, she hadn't found anyone willing to do it for long. Her gaze drifted to Derek, but she shook her head at herself. *Never going to happen.* Besides, he might be wanted for murder.

Zac walked up to them. "We were ready to let the cops know about it when Cal got that tingly sense he gets about a team member in trouble. We could see all your starts and stops that, frankly, didn't make much sense. He called Kieran, who thought you were a little squirrelly when you met up, so Cal sent us out here to check out the cabin and ensure you were okay. We were at the cabin when your SOS button went off. Who are these guys?"

"SOS button?" Derek asked, turning to her.

"We all wear one. I didn't have time to mention it, but I activated it before we left the SUV. I figured at least Secure Inc. could track us down if they took us."

"More likely they were going to leave you here dead," Declan called from where he stood by the bound guys. "They're not talking, but these guns look good and deadly."

Derek turned to Zac. "I don't know who they are either," he explained. "Though, I had a run-in with them earlier." He pointed to his face, and Roman snapped on a flashlight, only to shut it off immediately with a grimace. "They didn't tell me who had sent them, just that they wanted files. I assumed they were talking about the app that Hugo was working on.

I didn't even know that Hugo was dead until just about an hour ago."

Declan glanced up from his phone. "Cal's been updated. He wants us to return to Duluth, and he'll meet us at the station."

"Roger that," Roman said. "I want you and Zac to take Alayah and Derek back to Duluth in her SUV. I'll wait here for the police and then double back to where we parked ours."

"Cal wants everyone to return to Duluth together," Declan clarified, which made Alayah bite her lip. She didn't know too many people who didn't follow an order from Roman Jacobs. As Cal's foster brother, and a former FBI agent, he was second in command of the ship. Especially when Cal wasn't on site to assess the situation.

"Since he's not on the ground and I am, that decision falls to me. These guys are going to be in that SUV when the police arrive," he said, jabbing at the one behind her. "If we leave the vehicles unattended, someone else could swoop in and take them. I'd rather that didn't happen as I'm sure the police would as well. The faster we know who's signing their paychecks, the faster we get this solved so we can go home. Time is money and this is costing a lot of both right now."

"Yes, sir," Declan answered. Alayah was glad he was smart enough not to argue with him.

"All due respect, Roman," Zac said, to which Roman frowned. "If Zac and I go with Alayah and Derek, that leaves you alone and vulnerable. That's unacceptable. We all stay or we all go."

Roman dropped a hand on his hip as he glanced between the group. "Then we all stay. I'll have Cal send the circus to us. Might as well get comfy. We're going to be here for a while."

He walked off while Zac returned to help Declan with the guys coming around after taking a knock on the head. Weren't they in for a surprise?

Alayah turned to Derek. "When the cops arrive, I'm afraid they'll arrest you. I'm sorry."

"No apology needed," he promised, taking her hand gently. Now that the terror had drained away and their lives weren't at risk, she allowed herself a moment to bask in the warmth of his hand and the gentle way he caressed the back of hers. "You've gone above and beyond to help me tonight. If anything, I should apologize to you. It was wrong of me to involve you in my problems. You could have gotten hurt or killed. I didn't use my best judgment tonight."

"You're right," Declan said, walking up to them. "But neither did Alayah, even if her heart was in the right place. You have about ten minutes or less before the cops arrive. If I were you, I'd be sure your stories match. No lies. No half-truths. Just the whole truth and nothing but the truth. Got it?"

"Roger that," Alayah muttered as he walked away. Something told her this was going to be a long night.

Chapter Eight

Derek sat inside his cabin at his kitchen table, facing off with a detective from the Duluth Police Department. While they should have taken him to the station, they also didn't have any evidence that he had been the one to poison his boss. All they had was a water bottle that other people had come into contact with throughout the morning. He didn't have a lawyer present but had nothing to hide, so he agreed to answer their questions. They already knew he'd touched the water bottle, but proving that he'd put the antifreeze in it was another matter.

"You understand that you have the right to an attorney?" the detective, who introduced himself as Henry, asked.

"Understood," Derek agreed. "I don't have anything to hide, and I had nothing to do with Hugo's death. I didn't even know he'd died until a few hours ago."

"Walk me through what happened here," he said, motioning around the room.

Derek explained how he'd walked in on the guy ransacking his cabin. They'd found his bag in one of the black SUVs, so at least they had proof he wasn't lying about that. Not to mention the destruction to his face. "Once I got the upper hand, I ran," Derek finished.

"And that's when you ran into Ms. Heath? How do you know her again?"

"I don't know her, know her," Derek explained. The last thing he wanted to do was make it out as though he was using Alayah. Maybe he didn't know her well, but he did care about her and felt terrible that his situation put her in a position that might jam her up. "We met briefly at the convention center before I left earlier today. After escaping the cabin, I ran across the highway, and she almost clipped me with her car. I asked her for a ride when she stopped to check on me."

"And that's when she told you about your boss's death?" Detective Henry asked, taking notes on a pad in front of him.

"No, she didn't tell me. I found out when I saw a news story at a gas station. She was kind enough to let me ride with her to Two Harbors to escape the guys who attacked me."

"Maybe not the smartest move on her part," Henry muttered, to which Derek shrugged.

"Probably not, but it was kind. I was bleeding from my nose and couldn't see out of one eye. This," he said, motioning at his face, "is a thousand times better than it looked when she found me on the side of the road."

Henry's grimace was barely noticeable. As though he'd been taught to school his expressions.

"She gave me an ice pack and left me at the gas station in Two Harbors. That's where I learned that Hugo had died."

"Seems odd that you didn't call the police at that point," he pondered, to which Derek shook his head.

"Since I didn't know you were looking for me, why would I call you? The news just reported that the investigation is ongoing. It wasn't until Alayah picked me up again that I learned what actually happened."

"That's what I don't quite understand," Henry said, leaning back as though they were just having a friendly chat. "If you don't know her and she doesn't know you, why would she return? It's not like she could fight you off, and don't tell me that a woman with her condition doesn't consider that when she meets someone new."

Derek forced himself not to react to the detective's goading. What Alayah did last night would have been dangerous for any woman. They both knew it. That was why her trust in him mattered so much to Derek. It was also why he refused to tell Henry that Alayah had a gun in her vehicle. He had no idea if it was legal, and he was not going to get her or Secure Inc. into deeper trouble.

"If you want the answer to that question, you may have to ask her," he said evenly. "However, it may be that she didn't consider me a threat once she saw my face and I told her about the attack here. After she explained what happened to Hugo and that the police were looking for me, I agreed to return to Duluth and go directly to the police station."

"And she just took your word for it," he said again, as though he expected Derek to come clean that he'd been holding her hostage at gunpoint or something.

"Again, you'd have to ask her that question."

"So, you're on your way back from Two Harbors and decided to stop at the cabin one more time?"

"I asked her to drive past the cabin, mostly because I feared those guys would burn it down. When it was still standing, I convinced her to stop so I could run inside and get the evidence that would clear me."

"You had to know they would already have it, Derek,"

Henry said in that annoyingly placating tone they use as though they were trying to comfort you through your trauma.

"They'd have my bag, yes," Derek agreed. "I was the one who told him the files they wanted were in it, but they weren't in that bag. They were in my pantry in a safe that looked like a can of soup."

"That's a choice," the detective said.

"When you work for Hugo Victor, you learn ways to protect things that need protecting."

"A safe maybe?" Henry suggested. "Seems like that's what they're made for."

"They're also glaringly obvious in a place like this," Derek said. "A can of soup will be overlooked every time."

"Why even have it here?" he asked, leaning back as though that would take all the tension out of the room. "Why not leave it at the office? Or with Hugo?"

"The code is almost finished, and I planned to do some work on it while I was here. You never really go on vacation when you work for Hugo. You just do your work in a different place."

"He sounds like the kind of boss a person could grow to hate."

"I didn't hate Hugo," Derek said with a shake of his head, knowing those words were true when his heart constricted. "He ran a multibillion-dollar tech business and there were always a thousand moving parts. As his assistant, I was entitled to vacations that I never took for that reason. However, since he was supposed to be safely ensconced in a tech conference, it was the perfect chance for me to get away even if I had to do some work while I was here."

"In your cabin, which is conveniently located near Duluth."

"This cabin," Derek said, sitting forward to address the man, "has been here for three generations. There's nothing sinister about it."

"Other than the fact it's not deeded in your name. We know. We checked."

"You're correct. My mother owns it, and although I'm the only one who has used it since she moved to Florida, the deed won't come to me until she passes away. That's how it's always been. It wasn't like I was trying to cover my tracks. It's been that way since my grandfather owned the property."

"But it's sure convenient. Especially since no one at your office knew where you were staying either. Is that a coincidence, too?"

"No," Derek said, the one word coming out harsh. "That was on purpose. My vacation was none of their business. My job isn't like most other jobs in the company. The only person I report to is Hugo. Reported to," he said, correcting himself when he realized what he'd said. He was tired, sore, and this guy was getting on his nerves.

"What are you going to do now that the person you reported to is no longer with the company?"

"The thought hadn't even crossed my mind," Derek admitted. "Between the head-bashing, finding out the man I considered a friend was killed, and surviving an attempted kidnapping, I was more worried about my life than my job."

Derek saw the irony. Eight hours ago, he'd been determined to break away from Hugo and start his own tech company, certain that he could no longer give his all to someone other than himself. Now, he likely had no choice but to strike out on his own or return to working as a developer for Black Marlin Technologies. That wasn't a bad job, but still not the one that he saw for his future.

A man Derek didn't recognize walked through the door in a suit and tie while carrying a briefcase. He stopped by the table and stared down at the detective. "Are you finished with my client, Detective Henry?"

"Your client?" the detective asked, sitting forward again.

A card appeared in the man's hand, and he slid it across the table. "Ryland Frye, defense attorney. Excuse us for a moment."

Derek stood and followed the attorney to the other end of the kitchen. "I didn't call a lawyer."

"Cal Newfellow did. He asked me to stop by because whether you're guilty or innocent, you should never agree to speak to the police without representation present."

"I didn't kill Hugo Victor, and I have nothing to hide," Derek said, exhaustion cloaking him as he tried to make sense of everything, now nearly eight hours after taking several shots to the face with a fist. "I'm a lot of things, but I'm not a murderer."

Ryland walked over to the detective and stood before him. "We're done here."

"I'm not," Detective Henry said, standing and posturing before the lawyer.

"Maybe not, and that's your right, so either arrest my client or let him go. He's been attacked and needs medical attention as well as food and sleep. If the city wants to provide that for him, arrest him, and I'll meet you at the station to see your evidence."

The detective's face remained neutral, but Derek could see in his eyes that he was steaming mad to have their questioning interrupted. "He's not under arrest at this time." Derek heard the threat in the last three words. "The department must be informed of his lodging, and he cannot leave town. We may request formal questioning tomorrow at the station."

"All of which is acceptable," Ryland said, as though he was about to make friends with the detective. "Mr. Benjamin will remain in Duluth at the hotel connected to the convention center. He will be in room 2142 after his medical needs are attended to. Once he's had rest, he will be available to answer your questions. Now, if that is all, we'll be on our way."

Rather than wait for Henry to answer, Ryland grasped Derek's arm on his way past and walked him right out the door. Derek couldn't help but smile.

"Thank you," Derek said with all sincerity.

"Don't thank me. Thank Cal. He didn't want you to stay something incriminating because you were tired or had a head injury. The detective shouldn't have even requested a sit-down with you." He motioned for Derek to climb into a Mercedes SUV that looked very comfortable and very expensive. He checked his face for blood before he sat down, just in case. "I agreed to it," Derek said once they were on their way. "Doing anything else made me look guilty, I figured."

"Well, you figured wrong," Ryland said, glancing at him momentarily before looking back to the road. "If he thought for half a second that he had anything to hold you on, he would have arrested you immediately."

"He does have my fingerprints on the water bottle. That was kind of a sticking point for me, even though I didn't do anything other than what I normally do before every conference."

"While that's true, he also has Cal's fingerprints on it, and apparently two stagehands, but none of them have been arrested either."

"I didn't know that," Derek said with surprise.

"Of course not, because you were out here playing Daniel Boone while your boss was being murdered. Listen, I'm your counsel, so whatever we say privately goes no further than me. Before I formulate a plan, answer one question. Did you kill Hugo Victor?"

"Absolutely not!" Derek replied a little too loudly for his head. He rubbed his temple and sighed. "Sorry. I should have known you'd ask me that, but to hear someone think that you're capable of murder is offensive."

"As a defense attorney for twenty years, I assure you, everyone is capable of murder in the right setting and under the right circumstances, myself included. The man who has retained my services has killed more people than you have fingers and toes. For him, it was a necessary evil but one that weighs on him heavily, so he takes every chance he gets to help others."

"Cal doesn't even know me, though. We met briefly yesterday morning. That was it."

"Maybe Cal doesn't, but one Alayah Heath does, and apparently, she can be pretty persuasive when she wants to be."

Derek smiled as he stared out the window, a warm feeling creeping up from his cold toes. "Alayah put him up to this?"

"You didn't hear that from me. Everything equal, if you didn't kill Hugo Victor, then you'd better watch your step. Those guys who used your face as a punching bag aren't talking, so we don't know who hired them. If Cal tells you to do something, you do it without asking questions. Understood?"

"If it keeps me out of a jail cell and leads us to Hugo's real killer, I'll do anything he says."

Derek was never happier to see the city's lights on the horizon. He might not know Cal, but he was a fan for life thanks to Alayah. The thought of the feisty woman who drove a giant SUV while strapped into a booster seat made him smile. He was probably her fan for life, too.

Chapter Nine

Cal paced the hotel room while Alayah sat on the bed. He stopped in front of her with his hands on his hips. "What the hell were you thinking?"

"That someone needed help, and I should help him," she answered with a long-suffering sigh. It was hard not to make it sound like a question, but she stood her ground and didn't make excuses for her actions.

"Helping him would have been taking him to the ER or calling the police. What you did was reckless and dangerous!"

"Derek Benjamin was not and is not a threat to me, Cal," she said, shaking her head.

"You didn't know that!" he exclaimed, throwing his hands up in the air. "Good God, you picked someone up off the side of the road like some victim in a slasher movie!"

Alayah couldn't hold in her laughter. She was tired and worried about Derek, but sometimes Cal did get carried away without considering all angles. "Cal, I'm a thirty-two-year-old woman who's an excellent judge of character. Growing up the way I did, it was a skill I honed early on to protect myself. I could pick out the good and the bad, whether it was a doctor, teacher, or friend. I am not gullible or too trusting. Besides, there was a gun in the car, and I knew how to use it."

"Which you then gave to said hitchhiker!"

"Let's be so real right now, Cal. By the time I gave him that gun, he could have overpowered me thirty times and taken the car. All he wanted was the jump drive and a ride back to town."

"And you thought it was a good idea to lie to your boss about what you were doing?" He paused. "Your boss's boss, technically, but either way, what were you thinking?"

They'd been going through this same round of questioning for twenty minutes now, and she was tired. All she wanted was an update on Derek and a bed. There was no question that Cal had every right to be angry with her; she had lied to him, but he'd been the one to teach them to follow their gut instincts, and that's what she'd done.

"I'm sorry I lied to you on the phone, but Derek was already in the cabin when you called. We were heading back to town when he finished, so I thought it would be better to explain everything in person. In hindsight, that was the wrong choice, and you'd be well within your rights to fire me. I won't argue or fight you on it. I'll take my lumps for screwing up. My gut said Derek needed help, and I thought if I could get him back here, he could deal with the police."

"Why didn't you at least tell Kieran? He could have ridden back to Duluth with you. Been an extra set of hands."

"Because Kieran would have called you, and then it would have been a whole thing. I didn't want to spook Derek and have him run. I was worried that if the police found out I'd had him in my car and didn't take him to the police station, they'd arrest me or you or someone. I don't know!" She finally threw her hands up in frustration. "I thought I hit him with the car, Cal. What was I supposed to do? Everything got away from me. I'm sorry."

There was a knock on the door and Cal walked to it, sticking his eye to the peephole. When he pulled it open, the woman on the other side of the door was a sight for sore eyes.

"Selina!" she exclaimed as Secure Inc.'s nurse walked in and sat beside her on the bed. "What are you doing here?"

"Checking on you," she said, giving her a once-over. "Does anything hurt?"

"I'm fine," she said, her head tipped in curiosity. "Derek was the one who was hurt."

"Not according to him," Cal said, returning to stand by them. "And don't think I haven't noticed you limping on your left leg."

"Walk me through it," Selina said, kneeling on the floor and lifting her foot up. "It's swollen here," she said, pressing gently on the joint, which made Alayah hiss.

"Sorta got dumped out of the SUV and rolled on it when I fell. It stung for a minute, but then it was fine."

"No, it isn't fine." Selina opened her medic bag and pulled out an ice pack. She snapped it and then strapped it to Alayah's ankle with an elastic bandage before carefully swinging her leg up onto the bed. "You didn't notice the pain in it because the adrenaline kept you moving. It's clearly sprained. Tonight is ice and ibuprofen, and I'll reassess it tomorrow. If you have less pain, we'll brace it and keep you off your feet as much as possible. If it's more swollen or painful, we'll take you in for an X-ray."

"It really only hurts if I walk on it." Selina shook her head in exasperation as Alayah sighed. "You know what I mean. When did you get here?"

"We just rolled into town. Cal indicated my help was

needed here more than at Secure Inc." She glanced at Cal. "The package is on its way. It will arrive shortly."

"What package?" she asked, glancing between them. "It's almost two a.m. I've been up way too many hours, but even I know that no one is delivering packages at this time of night."

Cal crossed his arms over his chest. "Ryland is bringing Derek to the hotel. He's refusing to go to the ER, but he needs to be checked for a concussion and facial fractures."

"Who's Ryland, and why is he bringing Derek here?" she asked, her heart buoyed for the first time in hours. Once the police arrived, Cal had forced her to leave the cabin. She didn't know what had happened to Derek after that.

"Ryland is Secure Inc.'s lawyer. I sent him to pick Derek up at the cabin and bring him back here. The police don't have enough evidence to arrest him, but they are requiring him to stay in town as a person of interest."

Most of the tension left Alayah's shoulders to hear Derek wasn't being arrested. She had begged Cal to help him but didn't think he would. He probably shouldn't have, but she was grateful all the same. "Thank you, Cal," she whispered. "I know I made all the wrong decisions tonight, but I appreciate you listening to me about Derek."

"While I appreciate the apology, I don't think Derek had anything to do with Hugo's murder. That doesn't mean I agree with what you did," he said, holding up his fancy metal-and-plastic finger. "But until we can get to the bottom of this, we need him here, so we can ask questions and sort out what he knows."

"Now we're running our own investigation?" Selina asked, raising an eyebrow.

Cal crossed his arms again. "All I'm saying is, I don't

want to end up in a cell for touching a water bottle that killed a man. I'm certain Mr. Benjamin doesn't either."

"Unless he did it," Selina said, to which Alayah shook her head.

"While anything is possible, I find it highly improbable that he'd put ethylene glycol in his boss's water bottle and then go fishing less than twenty minutes from the murder scene."

"How did the antifreeze get in the water bottle then?" Selina asked. "Someone had to do it."

"That's the $64,000 question," he said, leaning against the television stand. "We'll poke around the security camera footage and our programs while the cops run down other leads. I'm not saying we're going to solve a tech billionaire's murder. I'm saying we'll make sure none of us end up in front of a judge for it."

"Fine, but not until everyone gets some sleep. You most especially," Selina said, turning to Alayah. "If you want that ankle to feel better, you must let your body rest."

"After I see Derek," she said, forcing as much conviction into her voice as possible.

"I'll check him out, and if I think he needs to go to the hospital, we'll get him there," Selina promised. "There's no need for you to worry about it. Sleep while you can. They'll need you to comb through those videos tomorrow."

"Not until I see Derek," she said again as Cal's phone beeped.

"He's in his room," Cal confirmed when he glanced up. "Alayah, get your walker, and I'll give you five minutes with him while I talk to Selina. Then, you sleep for at least five hours."

Well, great. The night just went from bad to worse. Not only had she picked up a stranger off the side of the road, but she broke another promise to boot. "I don't have my walker."

"What now?" Cal asked, hand on his hip. "Our agreement was that you took it with you everywhere, even if you don't use it."

"Cal, I had ten minutes from when I entered the doors of Secure Inc. until I left them again. My walker was in the back of the other car. I was so tired, I didn't even think about it."

"I did," Selina said, standing and walking to the door. Alayah's purple posterior walker sat in the hallway when she opened it. "We didn't find it until we cleaned out the SUV to head down, or I would have sent it with Kieran."

"Thanks, Selina," she said as she unwrapped the ice pack from her ankle and slipped her shoe back on. She could admit it felt a little better, so she'd make sure to put some ice on it while she was sleeping. At least the hotel would have an endless supply of it.

She grabbed the walker handles and pulled it around behind her to appease them, but there was no way she'd let Derek see her using it. She paused to ask herself why she cared if he saw her using the walker, but she already knew the answer. She was embarrassed. Should she be? No. She'd used a mobility aid for years and was never embarrassed or humiliated about it, but when it came to Derek Benjamin, she was. Later, she'd have to unpack the reason why, but that was a problem for another day when they didn't have a murderer to find.

"What's his room number?" she asked Cal.

"Selina will take you," he said rather than answer the question. "She wants to put eyes on him immediately before he gets too comfortable."

"I'll wait here for a bit and give her time to do that."

"As if," Selina said, holding the door open. "You'd ditch that walker the moment I turned my back."

They left her no choice, and as much as she hated to admit it, she was probably about to make her smartest move all night.

"Now that I'm standing again, I can see that I'm too tired to do anything more than take a shower and crawl into bed."

Selina offered her a sweet smile, telling her she knew exactly what she was doing but wouldn't say it in front of Cal. Alayah could be happy about that, at least.

Cal walked to the door before he stopped and looked at his watch. "We'll convene in our conference room at 0900 hours. Breakfast will be waiting."

That gave her six hours of sleep. Not ideal, but doable, so she nodded. "Wait, do we still have a room? Isn't the conference over?"

"Only postponed as of right now," Cal answered. "The organizers are waiting for the police to give them the go-ahead. They want to be sure this was an isolated attack before they proceed. Last I heard, they were considering reopening the conference around noon. Of course, they'd be using a different area for the presentations, but the police still need to clear the scene before letting anyone back in. I should know more in the morning."

"That's going to stretch us thin if we have to run security for the conference and try to comb through yesterday's situation."

"I agree, which is why I brought in more people. They'll run the conference if they restart it, while those of us who witnessed the murder will work in the background."

"I'll be there with bells on then," she said with a smile, fatigue washing over her.

"We'll let you get some sleep. Call me if you wake up

with more pain in your ankle," Selina said, and Alayah nodded in agreement.

"And for the record," Cal said as he started closing the door. "I may not like what you did tonight, but I respect you for following your gut and helping someone who needed it. In the future, I'd just prefer if you didn't lie to your only backup."

"Heard and understood, and I'm sorry for worrying you."

Once Cal and Selina left, she limped into the bathroom, leaving the walker by her bed out of defiance of the entire situation. As she stripped off her dirty clothes and turned on the water, Derek's face, all battered and bloodied, loomed in her vision. As hard as it was, she would do whatever was needed to avoid the man the rest of the weekend. He had been kind to her and ensured her safety to the best of his ability, but it would be too easy to fall for a guy like Derek. Good thing she was here to do a job and nothing else.

She glanced down at her body, which had more bruises than it had last night, but for the first time in her life, she found pride in herself for what she'd done to help Derek. She dried off and put on her pajamas, knowing that pride in her accomplishments would have to be enough for her. Falling for Derek was just asking for a broken heart.

Chapter Ten

When Derek made his way to the conference room the next morning, he felt much better. At least physically. This morning, the man in the mirror looked more like him than he had the night before. The pain medication Selina had given him, along with a hefty dose of prednisone, had brought the swelling under control and ended his headache. Selina had used medical glue on his split lip, which he'd appreciated because the hospital was not where he'd wanted to go. While his face still sported the bruises, and his lip was still fat, it would be a thing of the past in a few days. Overall, he looked like he'd lost in the boxing ring, but at least he was alive to tell the story. He could thank Alayah Heath for that. And he would, if he could find her.

Last night, when he asked Selina how she was, the answer was asleep, which was understandable. Selina told him Alayah had a sprained ankle after being dropped from the SUV, which sat like a lead ball in his belly. It wasn't fair that she got hurt helping him. He spent most of the night kicking himself until exhaustion finally pulled him into sleep for a few hours. The conundrum of who killed Hugo hadn't taken up residence because there was no way he was puzzling that out with his head pounding and half a concussion. Now that the light of day was here and he felt better, he'd do anything they asked of him. He wanted justice for Hugo, and to do that, they had to clear his name. Until they did, they couldn't focus on finding Hugo's killer.

Walking into the room, he homed in on Alayah immediately. She was sitting at a table with Cal and several guys, including Roman, the only one he remembered from last night. He promised himself that he'd keep it professional until he and Alayah were alone. He really wanted to find out how she was, but he wouldn't do it in front of everyone and risk embarrassing her.

"There's the man of the hour," Cal said. "Grab some breakfast and then join us." He motioned at the buffet. So, after a good-morning to everyone, he walked to the buffet and filled a plate. He was surprised by the spread the hotel had put up in the room. He was grateful to have hot food for his belly for the first time in almost a day.

Derek rejoined the team and sat in the only open seat… next to Alayah, who was trying her hardest to ignore him. If she didn't want to talk, he wouldn't push her. For all he knew, Cal had punished her for helping him last night. He doubted that, though. He may have given her a stern talking to, but the fact that she was sitting at the table told him she was still part of the team. He tucked into his breakfast as everyone else was also eating, so starting a conversation was pointless until everyone was done.

Unable to resist, he leaned toward Alayah slightly. "Thanks for your assistance last night with the lawyer. It made all the difference."

"That was Cal," she said, setting her muffin down and brushing off her hands.

"Not the way I heard it," he said, then popped more bacon into his mouth and waited for her to respond. She didn't. Apparently, he was on her blacklist even if no one else was mad at him. Sad as it made him, he'd have to respect her and not push. While he wanted to get to know her better, that didn't mean she felt the same way about him. He'd help with the investigation while he tried to earn back her respect. Maybe he didn't need that, but he wanted it because he had nothing but respect for Alayah Heath.

"We're waiting for the conference committee to decide if they're resuming the event, but the early indication I got was they will be," Cal said, leaning back in his chair. "They're going to move the presentations to a different theater. It won't hold as many people, but they don't expect any of the other speakers to draw the kind of crowd Hugo did, so they think it will work out fine. Sorry, Derek."

He held up his hand until he finished chewing. "No need to apologize every time you mention his name. I'm coping with his death by refusing to address those feelings until I've cleared my name and his killer is behind bars. It's the only way I can figure out how to keep my mind sharp and not focus on the grief and anger of losing a friend."

Cal nodded once. "When you have an analytical mind like you do, that's the best way to approach it. There will be time to grieve, but right now isn't the time. Now is the time to figure out who killed him. Grieving feels never-ending when a murder charge is hanging over your head."

Laying his fork down, Derek leaned in over the table. "For full disclosure, I planned to quit in January. Even before Hugo started feeling poorly, he was unable or unwilling to do much of anything for himself, which meant there was no such thing as time off. It's been three years since I've had more than one day to visit the cabin, and that was only because he was otherwise occupied. This would have been the first vacation I'd had since becoming his assistant five years ago. He only allowed it because I was less than thirty minutes away and could return quickly if he needed me. I expected to, just not for this reason."

"Wow," Roman said, shoulder-bumping his brother. "And I thought you were a taskmaster. Hugo was next level."

"Don't get me wrong," Derek said, holding his hands out to them. "There were no hard feelings between us. He paid me well for my devotion to him and the company, and I respected him for his contributions to the tech world, but it's a hamster wheel I can't run on anymore. I want a life that doesn't revolve around my work. Hugo had become a father figure for me, and fathers teach us a lot. In this case, he taught me that the last thing I want to do is wake up thirty years from now and be him. Someone with no family and no love in his life other than that which he paid for."

"Amen to that," Roman said. "There's the rat race, and then there's that."

"All of that said…" Cal lowered his voice as he leaned in over the table. "It's important that you play the grieving assistant as far as the official investigation."

"I am grieving, even if it's tempered," Derek said, his spine straight as he faced off with the team. "More than that, I'm angry that someone thought it was okay to kill someone I loved. It would have been much easier to hand in my resignation letter in January than to lower him into the ground in October."

Cal tipped his head in agreement before one of the other men asked, "Do you stand to gain anything from Hugo's death?"

"I'm sorry but I don't remember your name," Derek said when he turned to him.

"I'm Zac. We met last night in the woods, but it was

dark, and you were pretty jacked up. Your face looks much better this morning."

"Thanks for the assist last night, and as for my face, Selina is a miracle worker. Will I gain anything from Hugo's death? The answer is no. Since I worked for Hugo and not Black Marlin, with his death, I'll need to find a new job."

"Then who does gain from his death?" Zac asked the follow-up question he had been expecting but didn't know how to answer.

"That's information I'm not privy to, nor would I want."

"I'll get Mina on that," Roman said, taking out his phone and leaving the table as he punched in a number.

"Our plan for the day is to split up the work," Cal said now that everyone had finished eating. "Zac and Declan will go over the logs from our programs to see if we missed something, while Roman and I go through the security cameras and the logs from those tracking our movements. Alayah and Derek, I'm going to pair you together. Derek, I want you to tell Alayah everything you know about Hugo. From his shoe size all the way to who hated him and why. Every piece of his life should be accounted for on paper. Once that's done, go through the footage, looking only for Derek and Hugo from the time they arrived at the center until he collapsed. I want to know everywhere they went and who they talked to."

"Boss," Alayah said. "Maybe there's someone else better suited for that job. You'll need me to do the cloud work."

Derek could tell she didn't want to question her boss, but he also heard in her voice that she didn't want to work with him. He wasn't sure why, but once they were alone, he'd be sure to apologize for insisting she stop at his cabin last night. If she was in hot water because she helped him, he'd make it right.

"I made the assignments with thought to everyone's strengths, and I stand by them. I'll find you a place to work, which will be tricky since they're moving things around to reopen the conference."

"We can use my suite," Derek said without a second thought. "It has a large workspace."

"That would be great," Cal said. "Once Selina arrives, she'll need to check your face and Alayah's ankle, so having you together is ideal."

"Arrives?" Alayah asked in confusion.

"Selina and Efren had to stay offsite last night."

Derek had learned that Efren was Selina's husband and a member of Secure One. He was part of the new security team that would help with the convention while everyone else worked on clearing them.

Cal went on. "Normally, I would have brought Mobile Command, but there's no place to park a 45-foot motorhome down here. There were also no rooms available here, so they had to find one at a different hotel."

"How did I get a room, then?" he asked, glancing around the table. "They should have taken my room."

"Your room was booked for Hugo and had already been paid for," Cal said gently. "He hadn't checked in yet, so the police confiscated his belongings from behind the reception area and didn't need to do any evidence collecting in the room. It made sense to put you there since Hugo had already paid for the room."

"Okay, then they should have my room. It has a bedroom, a sitting area with a pull-out couch, and a work area. It doesn't make sense for one person to stay in it."

"Then you don't have a room, and as per the police, this is your home away from home until they rule you out as a suspect."

Alayah cleared her throat. "I could sleep in Derek's room on the couch, and you could use my room as the spare. Would that help?"

"That would solve the problem, but I won't ask you to give up your room," Cal said.

"You're not asking. I'm offering, as long as Derek doesn't mind." She turned to him, and he forced his expression to stay neutral even though he wanted to smile. "Is that a problem? I promise to stay out of your way when we aren't working, and it should be short-lived, right, Cal?"

"Should be," he agreed. "With any luck, we can all get out of here sooner rather than later. But at the very least, the conference ends in a couple of days, and rooms should open up."

"I'm happy to share the space with you," Derek said, keeping his voice even so she didn't hear *how* happy it made him to spend time with her again. "You won't be in my way. I owe my life to you, so this is the least I can do."

Cal clapped his hands together once. "With that sorted, I'll get the word out. Alayah, if you want to pack your things, I can have one of the guys deliver them to Derek's room."

"Don't be silly," Derek said, standing when Cal did. "I'll help her move her things, and once she's got the workspace set up, we'll hunker down."

"You good with that, Alayah?" When she nodded, Cal spoke again. "Once you're set up, text me. Roman and I want to understand Hugo's business model, so we'll sit in on that portion of your discussion, and then we'll leave you to your work."

With that, they headed out while Alayah scooted down off her chair and turned to him. "For the record, I don't want to do this, but I also don't want the rest of my team inconvenienced when everyone should be in the same place to make transferring of information easier."

Rather than wait for him to respond, she grabbed hold of a small walker that he hadn't noticed before and walked toward the exit with her head held high. He followed behind her, giving her the space she either needed or wanted to prepare herself to share a room with him. That was the least he could do, considering everything she was giving up to clear his name and help find Hugo's killer.

Chapter Eleven

Alayah's phone rang, and she glanced at it to see Mina's face on the screen. In the middle of packing her suitcase, she wanted to let it go to voicemail, but she also knew Mina had a reason for calling.

"I need to take this," she said, pointing toward the hallway, and he nodded as he wrapped cords to store in her computer bag. Leaving the walker behind, she stood in the hallway against the wall and answered. "Secure Watch, Alpha."

"Secure Watch, Whiskey," Mina said, her real name being Wilhemina. "How are you feeling this morning? I've been worried since Cal said you got hurt."

"Trust me when I say it was the most minor injury of my lifetime," she promised. "A barely sprained ankle doesn't count as getting hurt. I can do that walking down the hallway."

Mina's laughter filled her ear and made her smile. "That's fair, but you have to be careful. The last thing we want is to visit you in the hospital. Cal also gave me an update on what you were doing out there last night. That was a...choice."

Alayah knew she wasn't wrong, even if it rubbed her the

wrong way just a bit. "If I had a defense other than to say I was following my gut, I'd use it, but that's all I've got."

"My gut says your gut said Derek wasn't a killer, and he needed help, so you helped him. Is that accurate?"

"For the most part," she agreed. "When I looked into his eyes, he couldn't hide the fear there. Since it was a fair bet he didn't beat himself up, I opted to get him off the side of the road. The rest was unexpected."

"As I told Cal, that's what we teach you at Secure Inc. You're an educated, smart, sharp, calculating woman who was only doing what we taught you to do."

"You're saying you told him to chill out?" With Mina's chuckled agreement, she smiled. "I appreciate the assist. While he dressed me down, he made many good points, so I need to respect his position. It won't happen again. At least, not the lack of transparency like last night."

"We can't ask for more than that. All of that said, he also told me that he's paired you up with Derek to work on the Hugo angle. Do you have anything you need me to run down besides Hugo's beneficiaries?"

"Not yet," she answered, glancing at the door to her room. "We're just packing up my stuff to take to his suite, and then we'll get started. Hopefully, I can run down a lot of it from here, but if there's stuff above my pay grade, I'll get it to you immediately to start working on."

"Your room? His suite?"

Alayah explained the situation and waited for Mina to admonish her or lecture her on something…anything. She wanted Mina to confirm that it was a bad idea to work closely with him or to stay in a room with him. Then again, she already knew it was a bad idea, but she didn't see a choice considering the situation they were in. Ultimately, she had to do whatever she could to ensure Cal stayed out of jail. Did she want to be cooped up in a room with Derek for hours on end and sleep just feet away from him? Her brain said no, but the emotions coursing through her told a different story. There was something that drew her to him. She wanted to be his hero. That was the only way she could explain it.

Connecting with men was often difficult for her. She struggled with self-confidence around men but she didn't feel that way with Derek. It was natural, despite her prickly attitude this morning. That was out of simple self-preservation. Pushing him away was less painful than allowing him into her life only for her to get hurt. Self-preservation was no longer an option. Sure, she didn't have to agree to move to his suite, but she was also a team player, and there was no bigger team than Secure Inc. If she couldn't put her own fear and worries aside for her teammates, then she had a bigger problem on her hands.

"I see," Mina said when she tuned back into the conversation. "All I will say is, Derek may not be directly responsible for Hugo's murder, but we don't know that he isn't involved in some way, so be careful."

"I hear you loud and clear, boss," she promised. "You'll get frequent updates from me as we start mapping Hugo's movements."

"Good. If there is anything you want to hand off to us, do that. The sooner we can find something to clear Cal and Derek, the better. I can't have everyone tied up for weeks over there. As it is, we already owe you a week off, and this job isn't finished yet."

"I'll forfeit the week off as penance for not being a team player last night," she said, pushing herself off the wall. "You know I am and will continue to be. Don't worry about anything other than finding what we need to get out of this bind with life and reputation intact."

"Now that I can agree with," Mina said. "Keep me updated. Whiskey out."

The line went dead, and Alayah dropped the phone to her side and took a deep breath. She had to remind herself that no one was mad at her for her choices last night, and everyone had moved on. She should, too. That was going to be easier said than done when working so closely with Derek, but she'd put a smile on her face and put her best foot forward, which today was definitely not her left one. After checking it over, she made a mental note to ask Selina to come to Derek's room and wrap it for her so it wouldn't swell so much.

When she woke this morning and it was still sore, she resigned herself to using the walker, which meant Derek would see her with it. To his credit, he'd been nothing but helpful on the walk to her room, but she was still uncomfortable and embarrassed. That was definitely not her usual reaction. Any other day, she'd be straightforward about her mobility aids, but for some reason, she didn't want Derek to look at her as different from any other woman. Then again, she only needed the walker because she'd agreed to help him. While the walker revealed her dependence on it from time to time, it in no way indicated she couldn't clear his name and find Hugo's killer. And she had every intention of doing that.

Realizing she didn't have a key with her, she knocked on the door. When it swung open, he smiled, making his blue eyes light up from behind the shiner covering his right one. Selina had glued the split above his upper lip, so while there was still some swelling, it looked much better than it had last night.

"Thanks," she said as she limped into the room and grabbed the handle of her walker.

"Is everything okay?"

"Sure, sure," she said, walking to the bed to sit. "My ankle is just a little sore."

He knelt before her. "May I?" She gazed at him skeptically for longer than she should have before she nodded. When he lifted her foot into his hand, the tenderness of his touch hit her in places it shouldn't, but she was helpless to stop it. Growing up with her condition, she equated touch as either painful or necessary when it came to any medical situation. Her parents were her only source of loving touch. Even as an adult, there wasn't much tenderness of touch from anyone now that her parents didn't live close to her.

Derek touched her not as a fragile doll but as a woman, almost as though he understood her past experiences and wanted her to feel seen. Silly, since there was no way he could, but she liked it all the same. "It's very swollen. If we don't get this swelling down, Selina will insist on taking you to the hospital."

"The thought crossed my mind," she agreed. "It hurts but not like it is broken. She won't listen to me, though, considering."

"Considering what?" he asked, standing and walking to the dresser where the elastic bandage from last night was folded.

"My syndrome," she answered matter-of-factly. There was no sense trying to make it something it wasn't. Her syndrome was complicated and while her dwarfism was most obvious, it affected many other parts of her body, which made explaining it to people difficult. Especially when she didn't want to be written off as incapable. She was more than capable, but more often than not, it took her a long time to prove that. Much longer than it would take an abled woman. That was a shared experience in the disabled community, but even that knowledge didn't make it less frustrating.

Derek started wrapping the ankle with the bandage while he spoke. "What kind of dwarfism do you have?"

"It's called Ellis-Van Creveld Syndrome," she answered, staring at the wall so she didn't risk catching his eye as he worked. The last thing she wanted to see was that he felt sorry for her. Even if she could never have him, his pity would break her. "Along with other deformities, it causes short-limb dwarfism."

"I noticed your forearms and lower legs are a bit shorter than mine," he said as he secured the bandage.

"It would be hard not to notice," she agreed with a smile. "I have short forearms and fingers, and short lower leg bones."

"I would be lying if I said I'd heard of that syndrome before."

"That's not surprising since it's a rare one," she said as he slipped her shoe back on. It felt so much better already. "Thank you. I was going to ask Selina to do that since my T-Rex arms make reaching it difficult." She waved her arms in the air and roared.

He bit his lip but finally laughed as he dropped his hand to his hip. "That's not fair. I can't not laugh at that image."

"You're meant to," she said. "I use humor when I'm uncomfortable, and I'm extremely uncomfortable talking to you about this."

"Why?" he asked, tipping his head to the side but maintaining eye contact. "What do you think will happen? I'll stop liking you?"

"If you had grown up the way I did, you would know the answer to that question is absolutely."

His lips turned down in a frown as he knelt again. "My heart breaks that you've had that experience, but that's not me. The only reason I've ever stopped liking someone is because they showed me their true colors. That will never be the case with you. Last night, you showed me your true colors when you picked me up off the road, even though I looked like I had been mauled by a bear. That was all I needed to know about you, Alayah. Everything else has shaped who you are, but isn't who you are."

Her brows went up in surprise. "Why did it never occur to me to think of it that way?"

His shrug was lazy, but his gaze never left hers. "Because it's difficult to separate the two when you're mired in the pain of it. It takes work to be conscious of the line that separates them."

"That's fair. Speaking of fairness, I'm sorry for acting put out in the conference room earlier. Being a jerk is my other self-preservation technique when I feel vulnerable."

"You were being a jerk?" he asked, feigning surprise. "I didn't notice."

Her giggle made him smile, and a little piece of normalcy snapped back into place for her. All the noise inside her head quieted, and she could focus again on the steps that would lead her to find Hugo's killer and get her back to Secure Inc.

"Honestly, I was embarrassed about using the walker and didn't want you to see me with it." That wasn't easy for her to admit, but she wanted him to understand why she'd behaved that way.

"There's no reason to be embarrassed about something that helps you, Alayah."

"Truthfully, any other day I wouldn't be, but I didn't want you to see me as weak or incapable of helping to clear your name."

"I would never think that," he said with a shake of his head. She could tell he was upset that she thought he would. The idea that she'd insulted him got her right in the heart. "As for the walker, I love the purple glitter. It reminds me a little of your personality when you aren't being grumpy." He added with a wink, "I do have one question."

"Sure," she said, climbing off the bed and grabbing the walker handles. "Maybe I have an answer."

"Why do you pull it behind you as you walk instead of pushing it in front of you?"

She shook her head as she walked to the wall to unplug her charger and stow it in a bag. "It's called a posterior walker. It's normally used more for children than adults, but with my form of dwarfism, my chest is narrow and my ribs are short. That means leaning over on a walker like this," she explained, bowing her head, "makes it harder for my lungs to expand. Using the posterior walker ensures my posture stays upright, and I don't have any breathing issues. That said, I don't use the walker that much anymore unless I'm injured or sick. Cal and Mina require me to bring it on every remote job, just in case something happens."

"Like you get dropped from an SUV by some dude looking for the guy you stopped to help."

"Yep," she said with a smile. "Just like that. Now, with that out of the way, let's vacate this room and head to yours so we can set up and get this hunt for a killer underway. I'm sure you'd like to clear your name sooner rather than later and return to your life in…" She waited for him to fill in the blank.

"Minneapolis," he answered, holding the door for her

to walk through so he could grab her rolling suitcase and computer bag. "But I'd be lying if I said I was looking forward to returning to that life. Once I'm cleared of Hugo's murder, my life changes, and I don't have a clear picture of what it will look like. I do know it won't look like it did when I worked for him. When we left Minneapolis a few days ago, I already knew I'd outgrown my time there."

They walked to the elevator in companionable silence as she thought about what he'd said. Was she happy with her life? Would she want to change anything about it if the opportunity arose? When they stepped onto the elevator and he hit the button for the second floor, the answer was obvious. Derek reminded her that she led a solitary and sometimes lonely life. Would she love to find a partner to share her life with? Yes, but she'd learned a long time ago that the path to love was far too rocky for her to navigate. She'd have to find fulfillment in her work and leave the world of love behind.

Chapter Twelve

Derek stretched and snuck a look at his watch. They'd been working for an hour and a half but hadn't gotten very far. Mostly because it took forever to set up her equipment, which was copious, but he was grateful she had a full system on-site to work with. When she told him this was her travel system and he should see the one she used at Secure Watch, he couldn't help but smile. It was easy to picture her in front of four monitors while keeping track of the data on all of them without a problem.

"Do you have somewhere to be?" she asked as she sat on the desk chair that was retrofitted with the booster seat from her SUV. The desk wasn't low enough for her, so it was the only solution. Besides, it allowed her to prop her leg up and keep ice on the ankle. In an hour, Selina would check on them, and she wanted the swelling to be minimal so she wouldn't get hauled to the ER. A waste of precious time, if you asked her. He couldn't blame her. That was the last place he wanted to go. Thankfully, his headache had resolved, and his face no longer pounded with every beat of his heart, so he was on the upswing.

"The only place I have to be is here. Is Cal on his way?"

"They should be here momentarily. Have you heard from the detective this morning?"

"Nope, but I don't expect it to stay that way, which is another reason to get this sorted as quickly as possible. I could be hauled in at any moment for that formal interview they threatened me with last night."

"If they had anything on you, they would have done it already," she said. "Now they know you have a good lawyer, which means they can't try to use fear against you. They'll have to do the police work before they can bring you in, which takes time."

"I hope you're right," he said as there was a knock on the door. He walked to it and, after checking the peephole, pulled it open for Cal and Roman. They were formidable men, and he could see why they ran a successful security business. He certainly wouldn't mess with them and he was never accused of being small himself.

"All set up?" Cal asked as they walked in.

"Ready to go, boss," Alayah said. "Derek was just about to give me the breakdown on Hugo's business."

"Right," he said, hand in his hair as he tried to put his thoughts in order so it would make sense to someone who didn't live in his world. Roman and Cal grabbed chairs from the table and sat. "Hugo owned the business but had a four-person board he worked with."

"Does the board hold any shares?" she asked as she typed, but he shook his head.

"No. Hugo maintained full control of the business. At least, he did the last I heard."

"Which means Hugo called the shots and the board was along for the ride? Not sure I understand the need for a board then," Cal said.

Derek made a so-so gesture as he walked toward Alayah. "Hugo had control of the business in terms of money, but he created a board to help keep him in check."

"I don't understand if it was his business," she said, turning to him, and he was once again struck by her beauty. Her bright smile made her blue eyes sparkle, and her petite nose sat above the perfect pair of kissable lips. He'd likely never have the chance to kiss them, but that didn't change the fact that he wanted to.

"Okay, so Hugo was known for his—" he motioned his hand around in the air, looking for the right word "—impulsiveness. He liked shiny new things, but they quickly became dull once he started working on the project and realized it would take longer than overnight to complete."

Roman spoke up. "You're talking about apps or something else?"

"Yes, apps and programs that interested him or that he heard about at a conference or in a magazine. Hugo was brilliant but extremely ADHD, and I mean that was a medical diagnosis he carried."

"Is that why he set up a board to keep himself in check?" Cal asked and Derek nodded.

"He was self-aware enough to know that jumping from one thing to another without finishing anything wouldn't make for a lasting business plan."

"That's kind of the nature of the beast with ADHD, though," Alayah said. "Not finishing things is the struggle."

"Fair, but Hugo could focus when he wasn't given a choice. Hence, the board. They had monthly meetings to discuss Hugo's latest inspiration, programs and apps that were in progress within the company, as well as ones that were nearing completion and going to marketing. Then they'd discuss what project they'd start next. Sometimes, it was a unanimous decision, while other times, it required negotiation until an agreement was reached. At least, that was how it was during my first year as his assistant. I always sat in on the monthly meetings to take notes because Hugo was often lost in thought. He would forget the finer points of things they'd talked about."

"And after the first year?" Cal asked as Alayah typed.

"The company was already a multimillion-dollar company when I joined it, but around the second year I was his assistant, he sold several apps for billions of dollars each. Suddenly, the company hit the *Forbes* list, and that changed the landscape. Hugo was less involved in the day-to-day coding and app development, and he had the financial freedom to work on his own little pet projects while his app developers worked hard to keep the business solvent."

"What are the board members' names?" Alayah asked with her fingers on the keyboard.

"Curtis Clemons, Joel Hill, Salma Barker and Charlie Grant."

"And Hugo made five," Roman said. "Was that so there was always a tiebreaker, or was it so Hugo's vote could always be nullified?"

"I can't answer that, though I suspect a bit of both," Derek said. "Hugo had big dreams, as is obvious by the way Black Marlin Technologies has become one of the largest companies in the tech industry outside of Silicon Valley." Alayah rolled her eyes, which made him curious. He'd have to ask her about that later.

"Black Marlin Technologies. That's an interesting name for a company in Minnesota," Cal said. Derek wasn't surprised that he'd pick up on something so subtle.

"Hugo was fascinated by black marlins. They're the most sought-after fish but the most difficult to catch. They're also giants of their ocean. That's what he wanted to be. Sought after, difficult to catch, and a giant in the business. And he was, until yesterday."

For a moment, that overwhelming grief for the man who had become like a father to him, despite all his flaws, overtook him. In hindsight, a fresh understanding dawned on him about how important Hugo was to his life. He cleared his throat to force away the emotion, so he could focus on helping Secure Inc. find Hugo's killer.

"If I understand this correctly, we have four other suspects in Hugo's murder," Alayah said, giving him a moment to collect himself, for which he was grateful.

"I guess?" Derek asked. "But Curtis flew to California two days ago, so he's certainly not in Duluth. I don't know about the rest of the board, but I would assume they're at the office working."

"It's only a hair over two hours from Minneapolis to Duluth," Roman said. "An easy trip to make without raising anyone's suspicions or anyone even noticing their absence. We need to track their whereabouts over the last two days. Curtis included."

"He's in California," Derek said adamantly. "I drove him to the airport, so he doesn't even have a car."

"Did you see him board?" Cal asked, and Derek shook his head. "Then you don't know that he's in California. Where can you rent a car?"

"The airport," Derek answered with a groan. "It's not Curtis. He doesn't stand to gain anything by killing Hugo."

"That you know of," Roman said, holding up a finger. "Until we know who gains control of the company after Hugo's death, we must look at everyone in the company. Including yourself."

"I have no secrets," Derek assured them. "Do you want my social security number? You got it. Do you want my phone records? I'll call and get them for you. Do you want my banking records? I can show you those right now."

Cal held up his hand to stem his angry words. Actually, they were more desperate than angry. "Listen, son, I want you to understand that we're not trying to pin this on you. Just the opposite is true. At the very least, we need to prove that you have no financial gain from Hugo's death."

"I don't. I'm now unemployed, so I'll have to take a lower-paid position within the company, if they'll rehire me, or move on."

"Mina is working to learn who gets controlling power for the company now," Roman said.

Derek shrugged. "I would assume it's Curtis or the entire board for a period of time. That's how it's usually done so that things can continue to run smoothly in the interim. From there, I would think the company would be sold via the terms are stated in the will."

Alayah paused her typing to turn to him. "You don't think Hugo would just leave it to someone in the company?"

"It doesn't work that way in business," Derek said. "Though…" He frowned, and Cal motioned for him to spit it out. "The board members have a salary, but they don't have shares in the business. Hugo owns the business himself. Owned the business himself," he corrected.

"Which means while you may not be privy to who the company goes to upon Hugo's death, the board might be."

"Maybe, but I just remembered an argument that broke out at the last board meeting. Honestly, it was the reason Hugo agreed to speak at the conference. He wanted to get away from the office for a few days and decide how to approach the matter."

"Was it a serious argument or something minor that could be easily fixed with open communication?" Cal asked.

"This was the most serious argument I'd ever heard in

that boardroom. The board wanted to take the company public, but they couldn't do that without Hugo's agreement."

"And Hugo didn't want to do that?"

Derek shook his head as he bit his lip. "He threatened to fire them all and said the only way they'd get his company was—"

"Over his dead body," Alayah finished, and he nodded.

"Looks like they got their wish," Cal said.

Derek didn't want to believe that one of the people he worked closely with every day was responsible for Hugo's murder. Then he remembered what Ryland had said last night in the car. Everyone was capable of murder in the right circumstance.

They might have just found their motive.

Chapter Thirteen

Derek inhaled deeply as he stood on the hotel balcony. Fresh air was exactly what he'd needed after a long day of making lists and questioning everything he knew about the man he'd worked with for years. When the conference had resumed as promised, he and Alayah had stayed in his room to hunt down the Black Marlin Technologies board members. All had been accounted for in Minneapolis except for Curtis, who was accounted for in California at the time of Hugo's murder. Upon hearing of Hugo's death, he took the four hour flight back to Minneapolis. Derek expected a call from him soon. Was he dreading it? Yes. He expected to be blamed for Hugo's death.

The terse text he'd received from Curtis saying he'd be calling was enough for Derek to question his choices. Rather than guess, he called Ryland for advice. Should he even talk to him, or should he let his calls go to voicemail? Ryland suggested he answer and get a feel for the temperature at the main office. There was little Curtis could do to him, so he should approach the call calmly but not offer any information that wasn't already public knowledge.

While he waited for the call, he worked on compiling a list of anyone with deep enough pockets to purchase Black Marlin Technologies. Derek was certain it wouldn't be Curtis or anyone else on the board. They didn't have the capital. Hugo was unlikely to leave the company to a single individual, but the possibility existed that he would leave it to the board as a whole. If that happened, the board would take the company public and protect everyone's job. He understood their argument, but he also saw Hugo's side. He'd started the company with nothing and had built it into what it was today. Hugo knew that taking a company public was often a nightmare scenario that destroyed friendships, not that his refusal not to hadn't resulted in possibly the same thing.

Hugo had told Derek on the way to Minneapolis that he was making plans for semiretirement. He wanted to live a little before he was too old to enjoy a sunset cruise in Alaska or the company of a beautiful woman. Had that surprised him? Yes. Honestly, he figured his boss would work until he'd had a heart attack on the job. Ironically, he had, but it wasn't of his own doing. It left Derek to wonder who else knew about his retirement plans. Hugo never came out and said he was selling the company, but it wasn't a business you could give only part-time attention to. He would have to sell or hand over his control of the business to someone else for it to run smoothly. Suddenly, Derek wished he had asked more questions. He'd just thought it was Hugo being Hugo, and there was no way the man who was so consumed by work would ever walk away from it.

Thinking back over the last few years, he could see Hugo moving toward retirement. He attended fewer conferences and was less excited about every little development that came across his desk. He relied on Derek to keep things running while he took long lunches and early dinners. Maybe that was why he had started to feel so jaded about his work over the last year. His work had frequently become him doing Hugo's work. He stood up straight on an inhale. Why hadn't he thought of that until now? Maybe because when in the trenches, a person didn't see anything around them until they climbed out.

His phone rang, and he glanced at the number, taking a steeling breath before answering. "Curtis," he said as a greeting. "Thank you for getting back to town so quickly."

The man on the other end was silent momentarily. "I'm still in shock. What the hell happened?"

"I wish I could tell you," Derek admitted. "We did the same thing we do for every conference."

"But somehow, a lethal dose of antifreeze ended up in his water? The water you poured into the bottle?"

Derek had already braced himself for the accusation, but it still hurt to hear it from someone he'd worked so closely with. He was not about to discuss this with him, as Ryland warned him the call may be recorded. "I don't know when I'll be able to return to the office," he said instead. "It could be a week, but hopefully less. Once I'm cleared to leave town, I'll head back."

"Whatever for?" the man asked, disdain lacing the two words. "Your employment here has been terminated based on Hugo's death. Your personal effects will be shipped to your house."

"I see." Derek had been prepared for that scenario, but it still hurt. He had considered them friends and had hoped they'd look out for him. He would get his final pay, as per his contract, but then he'd be on his own. "Maybe we should sit down and talk about this. You may need my help until Hugo's will is read and the business secured."

"As though we'd need help securing the business from a glorified secretary. I think we can manage while Hugo's lawyer sorts out his wishes. You may leave your work computer and phone at the front desk. Your credentials have been pulled, so don't bother trying to log in."

"Since the Duluth Police Department has my work computer and phone, they may have an issue with being unable to access them. I'll be sure to let them know who to call. Goodbye, Curtis."

He jabbed the red button on his phone in anger and groaned, letting his head fall back to face the sky. In the span of a five-minute phone call, he had become a pariah in the industry, and there was nothing he could do to change that. Forget starting his own company. No one would touch him now.

ALAYAH KEPT AN EYE on Derek through the patio doors from where she sat on the bed, icing her ankle. Selina had stopped by after they'd arrived at the hotel to check on her. Satisfied that it was a simple sprain they could manage with ice and an elastic bandage, Selina had agreed she didn't need to see the doctor. Since Alayah couldn't wear an adult-sized ankle brace, and Selina didn't have access to anything smaller, she had no choice but to use the elastic bandage. That meant she had to allow Derek to help her rewrap it whenever it had to be removed for icing. It also meant having his hands on her body. That sent tendrils of heat through her, even if his touch was innocent.

The biggest thing she'd learned about him today was that he had no reason to kill his boss. Not that she ever thought he had, but when she'd listened to him speak about Hugo and heard the emotion that laced each word, she'd understood that Hugo was more than a boss to him. Derek would most certainly mourn Hugo's loss. Their relationship had begun as a working one, which over time evolved into a more father-and-son-like relationship. Derek had told her multiple stories about helping Hugo out with projects he needed done at home. That wasn't part of his job description, but he'd said he knew Hugo couldn't do it alone. While he could afford to hire it done, sometimes it couldn't wait, so Derek had stepped up. Hugo had told him that he was the closest thing he ever had to a son, and he was so grateful for him.

It was for that reason she suspected he had struggled so much with the decision to leave Black Marlin Technologies for greener pastures. He was worried about leaving Hugo, knowing their relationship was special and Hugo was unlikely to find someone like Derek again. Part of her also wondered if he was worried about Hugo's mental health. Derek had mentioned several times that Hugo had been forgetful recently, and his health seemed to be worsening. He'd encouraged him to see his doctor, but Hugo had refused. Despite that, Derek was worried enough to go behind his back and schedule a doctor's appointment next week. An appointment that came too late.

She could tell something had changed when he walked back through the patio doors. The fight had gone out of him after that phone call, and she suspected Curtis had thrown around accusations that he'd killed Hugo.

"How did that go?" she asked, removing the ice from her ankle.

Rather than answer, he tossed the phone on the bed and started to rewrap her leg without her asking. When he was finished, he sighed. "He told me my employment was terminated since Hugo is dead. My personal effects will be sent to my home, and my credentials are revoked. I have no place there anymore."

Frowning, she stood up on the bed and wrapped her arms around his neck in a hug. "I'm sorry."

When he wrapped his arms around her, she leaned into him, the hug doing as much for her as for him. "He called me a glorified secretary and said my time with Black Marlin was done."

"I guess this is your chance to break out and start your own company without guilt," she said, running her fingers through the soft hair at the nape of his neck. She swore he shivered, but she couldn't be sure.

He leaned back with a smile and helped her sit again before he sat beside her on the bed. "Unfortunately, that phone call tells me that ship just sailed. I can start my own company, but no one will want to work with me if they think I had something to do with Hugo's death. If Curtis starts spreading lies about me, my time in this business will be over."

Alayah hoped that would be the worst of his problems. She wondered if it had crossed his mind that he could still be arrested for Hugo's murder. He grasped her hand in his, as though it was the only thing keeping him from drowning. She glanced at his handsome face, now marred with a frown, and she vowed to do whatever was necessary to prove his innocence. If she couldn't, he could lose a lot more than his job.

Chapter Fourteen

"Derek—" she started to say just as her phone rang. *Cal*, she mouthed before she answered. "Secure Watch, Alpha."

"Secure One, Charlie. Is Derek there?" Cal asked.

"Yes, he's right here."

"Put me on speaker. I have a question."

She hit the button. "Go ahead."

"Derek, have you ever heard of a company called Virtual Scorpion?" Cal asked, and the man beside her let out a sarcastic laugh.

"Who hasn't heard of Virtual Scorpion?" he asked instead.

"Well, I hadn't until Mina mentioned them as a potential direct competitor of Black Marlin Technologies."

"There's nothing potential about it," Derek said. "Virtual Scorpion is Black Marlin's direct competitor. Josh Hunt has been a thorn in Hugo's side for the last ten years. He wasn't even a light in his father's eye when Hugo started his company, but Josh is convinced his youth puts him above Hugo's knowledge in this industry. He's wrong, which Hugo proved time and again. Black Marlin's apps are far better suited for their intended users, and we got them to market faster and with better results than Josh could ever hope to accomplish."

"I'm hearing one word there," Cal said. "Motive."

Derek was silent for a moment. "Wait, you think Josh Hunt had something to do with Hugo's death?"

"I have to think that," Cal explained. "Especially after I checked the conference roster to discover that Josh Hunt of Virtual Scorpion is doing a presentation on Sunday to discuss the same kind of app that Hugo was presenting."

"That's somewhat accurate. They're both cybersecurity apps but otherwise vastly different."

"The explanation will probably be over my head, but I want you to give the team a rundown on your experience with Virtual Scorpion. I'll patch Mina in by video conference. She can start looking via her contacts for any interactions between Virtual Scorpion and Black Marlin that may have occurred before you started working for Hugo. Should we meet in the conference room in thirty?"

Alayah knew Derek needed some time to gather himself after the phone call with Curtis, so before he could answer, she took it off speaker and held it to her ear. "We haven't eaten in hours. Can you give us sixty to get something to eat and some fresh air? We're both a little tired and punch-drunk."

Whatever Cal heard in her voice must have told him there was more to the story, so he agreed to meet them in an hour in the conference room. She hung up and turned to the man still sitting beside her as he stared out the window.

"What's funny is, last night, when those guys attacked me, the first person who came to mind was Josh Hunt. I wondered if he was behind it, but I couldn't get there with him killing Hugo over an app. I should have thought to mention it to Cal."

"You should have thought about all the people who might

want your boss dead when you've been attacked twice and nearly taken hostage, then accused of your boss's murder?"

"Well, when you put it that way," he said, his lip tilting upward a little. "It has been a day."

"I do think we should make a list of other companies that might be interested in buying Black Marlin Technologies before we meet up with them."

"I've been thinking about it, but there aren't many that have the drive or the capital to buy out Black Marlin, but I'll keep thinking. If you're hungry, we should get some food."

Alayah took his hand and rubbed her thumb across his knuckles to comfort him. "That was for Cal's benefit. I wanted to give you some time to recover from the phone call with Curtis before you had to jump into the next thing. It's okay to take a minute to breathe in the middle of this awful situation."

His nod told her that was exactly what he needed. It was heavy and laced with an intense sadness for what he'd lost over the last twenty-four hours. "It's hard to find an empty slot to stick the hits that keep coming."

"Derek, you lost someone you were close to for many years. You're human, so it's natural to feel a little bit lost and, in this situation, worried."

"I am worried, but you're the reason I'm sitting here alive, Alayah. I don't know what I'd do without you and Secure Inc. helping me. Probably be behind bars, and going down for Hugo's murder. It still hasn't sunk in that he's dead. I keep expecting him to call and update me on his day."

"I wish with all my heart that things were different, Derek. There's nothing I can do or say that will make this any easier, but I'll be here for you if there's anything you need."

He leaned down and touched his forehead to hers. "Being here and fighting for me, even though you're scared of whatever this spark is between us is everything. When this is over, I want to keep seeing you."

"Derek, you don't want to—"

He put his finger on her lips. "Don't tell me what I want or don't want, Alayah. Tell me what you want."

The words stuck in her throat as she gazed up at him, his blue eyes hooded as he waited, a hairsbreadth from her lips. She had a decision to make. Offer this man a life preserver in the middle of a stormy sea or protect the wall she'd built around her heart. Intuitively, she knew she couldn't do both. Picking him was a surefire way to a broken heart. Then she thought about how broken he already was, and she wanted to be the balm to help soothe him. Cupping his face, she brought his lips to hers.

He didn't hesitate. His lips took over, brushing hers in a gentle, close-lipped tease of getting-to-know-you like she'd never experienced before. First kisses were usually awkward and uncomfortable, but not this one. She'd only known him mere hours, but his kiss felt like walking in the door after a long day and knowing you were home. That you were safe. The very thought drew a whimper from her, and he caressed her cheek with his thumb, as though he knew she needed to feel safe as she opened herself to him. She'd never kissed a man with such tenderness before. That was when she realized she'd never opened herself so completely to the other men she'd been with. Her heart never allowed it. With Derek, it wouldn't let her hold back. That was terrifying beyond belief but also, oddly enough, freeing. His kiss, touch and words told her she was safe with him for however long they were together.

She broke the kiss first, reaching to trace his lips. "I'm

sorry. My low lung capacity makes long kisses more difficult." While she wanted to look away in embarrassment, the honesty in his gaze wouldn't allow it.

"Don't apologize. I only have two words to say. Thank you," he whispered, his thumb caressing her lower lip.

"For what?" she asked, the sensation of his skin on hers sending a skitter of desire down her spine.

"For trusting me. For offering me comfort when the very idea terrified you. For showing me that this thing I'm feeling in here," he said, running his fist up and down his chest. "It's real and you feel it, too. Does that scare you?"

"Strangely enough, no. For the first time in my life, you showed me the door marked Hope instead of the one marked Fear. So even if we never kiss again and you disappear from my life, what you gave me in that kiss will stay with me forever. I've spent so long walking in fear that I never once considered what hope might feel like. For that lesson, I'll always be grateful."

As though hope was all he needed, the fear in his eyes disappeared as he wrapped her in his arms. "Sweetheart, the last thing I want to do is disappear from your life, so I'm going to fight like hell to prove my innocence. I want nothing more than to keep kissing you."

She gazed up at him, a shy smile on her lips. "Prove it."

And he did.

Chapter Fifteen

The conference room was quiet when they walked in, other than the tapping of keys as the team searched through the footage to prove Derek and Cal were innocent of Hugo's murder. He was struggling to bring his mind back around to clearing himself after kissing Alayah. It wasn't just the kisses that had blown him away, though. It was the kisses followed by the twenty minutes she'd let him hold her in silence and just breathe. She'd given him twenty minutes with no phones ringing and no one demanding something of him. It was the time he needed to remember the man he'd lost as someone he loved, even if he was demanding. There was nothing truer of geniuses in general, and Hugo certainly was one. That was the reason others, including Josh Hunt, wanted to copy his every move.

The kiss had unlocked a new worry. That she would be ripped away from him now that he'd found her. When she was in his arms, he could put aside everything else and remember there was still hope in the middle of this mess. He wanted to ask her to share his bed tonight, for comfort only, but he figured that would be a tough sell. He believed that intimacy had nothing to do with sex, and while it could occur during lovemaking, it also existed without it. To him, true intimacy was opening yourself on a deeper level than required for casual sex. It was showing the other person your demons and letting them decide if they were ones they could accept. Sex, when consensual, only requires you to open your body. Intimacy, on the other hand, requires opening your soul.

He'd gotten a taste of that in the hotel room a bit ago, and now he craved it. He craved the comfort it offered him as he rode this Tilt-A-Whirl of uncertainty. Would he feel this way if someone else were helping him? No, because no one else was Alayah. She was vivacious, intelligent, open and sometimes brutally honest. After the kiss they'd shared, he somehow knew nothing would ever be the same again.

Cal walked in with Roman, and everyone turned in their seats to give them their undivided attention. Derek knew the team respected their leader, but of all the interactions he'd witnessed thus far, it was more than respect. It was love. They all loved each other and wanted to pull their own weight in keeping Secure Inc. above reproach in every job they did.

"Sorry for the late hour, but our digging revealed questions only Derek can answer for us. I want everyone to have the same information as we branch out in our search, so I've asked him to walk us through it. Before we do that, how did the conference go for you today? Any hang-ups? Do we need more help?"

The man introduced to him as Efren was the one to answer. "We're good on the security end of things, boss. The organizers brought in extra personnel to scan bags for weapons before attendees entered the lectures, which frees us up as security guards for the speakers. There's only tomorrow left, correct?"

"Tomorrow and the final speaker on Sunday morning, who will close the event," Cal said.

"The man of the hour, Josh Hunt," Derek muttered sarcastically, to which Alayah snickered from where she sat beside him.

"From the tech side of things, it's easygoing," Zac said. "Bringing Delilah in to replace Alayah was helpful and gave us plenty of coverage so one of us can be working on the cloud while the other two are running the conferences. We noticed that tomorrow there are three panels rather than individual speakers, so that will be a more intimate setting."

The word conjured an image that heated the back of Derek's neck, but he forced himself to stay in the game and not let his mind drift to holding Alayah all night long.

"We'll sit down and make a plan for those panels tonight," Cal agreed. "The final speaker for Sunday morning has a heavy footprint, so we'll need a tight leash on that one. The speaker is Josh Hunt, owner of Virtual Scorpion Productions. As he's Black Marlin's direct competitor, Derek is here to tell us about Josh's dealings with Hugo Victor."

Cal walked over and handed him a marker to use on the whiteboard at the front of the room.

"Thanks, Cal. As he said, Josh owns Virtual Scorpion Productions out of Chicago. He's young at barely thirty-five, but highly ambitious, and he set his sights on Hugo Victor immediately after graduation from college. He worked as an intern for Black Marlin Technologies for a few years after graduating from Caltech."

"Seriously?" Cal asked, and Derek nodded.

"And he was good. Probably one of the best interns Black Marlin has ever had, myself included." That got a chuckle from around the room. "But he was a little too ambitious. Josh tried to insert himself into projects he didn't belong in and ended up costing Hugo a pretty big sale when he promised a client something he couldn't deliver. Understandably so, Hugo was upset and let him go."

"Giving Josh a reason to harbor a grudge," Roman deduced.

Derek gave a nod. "Essentially. He moved to Chicago and started his own company with the help of Daddy's money. Whenever he saw Hugo at events or conventions, he kept their interactions friendly, but a low level of hatred always simmered beneath the surface. At least on Josh's part. Hugo was never bothered by Josh's snark until he started trying to one-up his apps."

"Were there copyright violations involved?" Roman asked, but Derek shook his head.

"No, because you can't copyright public domain ideas, right?" he asked as everyone nodded. "It was more like he'd find out what Black Marlin was working on, and he'd immediately start working on his own version of it."

"Josh was the great impersonator," Roman said, and Derek pointed at him in agreement.

"That, but he struggled to get the notoriety he thought would come with following in Hugo's footsteps."

"Except he wasn't," Alayah pointed out. "He was copying his footprints, and Hugo had bigger feet."

Derek touched his nose. "Ding, ding. Unfortunately, that concept was not one Josh could grasp. Instead, he doubled down and doubled down until, suddenly, Hugo was almost an obsession for him. We had to start heavily vetting new employees to ensure they weren't tied to Josh or sent as spies to report back. The app Hugo planned to promote at this conference was one that the two of us created together Even the board didn't know about it until that ill-fated board meeting earlier this month. It was our little side quest, so to speak. We had a lot of fun creating the app together, and all that was left was for Hugo to put the final touches on his coding and then test it. But we never intended to sell it, despite the hundreds of times Josh asked to buy it. We intended to allow vulnerable institutions to use the app to protect themselves. Institutions that couldn't afford companies like Secure Watch to protect their assets or people. Places like nonprofit hospitals, clinics and low-income school districts."

"Admirable," Cal said with a tip of his head. "The need is there, and honestly, there aren't enough of us in this business to go around, so many people depend on these apps to remain part of the business landscape."

"Agreed," Derek said. "It just hit me that I'll never see that happen now. The board didn't like our plan, but Hugo still owned the company and could do what he wanted with something he created on his own time and his own dime." He cleared his throat rather than continue to speak, and Alayah jumped in.

"Derek heard from the head of the board this afternoon. Curtis informed him that since he was employed and paid by Hugo rather than the company, his work with Black Marlin Technologies was over."

Cal raised an eyebrow. "That's brutal, but maybe not unexpected?"

"No, not unexpected, but what was unexpected was his belief that I was responsible for Hugo's death. I get it. His friend is dead, and he wants someone held responsible for that. I'm not that person, but I'm the easiest person to take his anger out on. I'll shoulder that for Hugo's memory, but I'll never work in the industry again because of it."

Cal walked over and squeezed his shoulder, giving him a moment to compose himself. "Secure Watch will always have a place for you, Derek. We don't allow great talent to walk away if we can help it. Don't make any decisions until this mess is cleared up and you've had time to think without the threat of arrest hanging over your head. Okay?"

"Thanks, Cal," he said with the utmost sincerity. It was easy to see why Cal's team was so dedicated to him. He cared.

"I also think that whoever is behind Hugo's murder may plan to use me as their scapegoat."

"Can't say the same thing didn't run through my mind," Cal said.

"I just can't get behind it being someone I worked closely with, or even Josh. I'm sure that's delusional, but I'm a newbie at being accused of murder."

"It's only delusional in the sense that you're a good person who believes the same of others," Efren said. "Misguided may be a better word, but that's why you have us on your team. You need that when you're too close to a situation."

"Agreed," Roman said. "So, we have Josh Hunt as a Hugo hater. Anyone else?"

Derek walked to the whiteboard and wrote two names. "Granite Intelligence," he said, tapping the name. "Hugo had a run-in with their CEO, Marcus Bonner, at a conference about three years ago now. They were trying to sell an app that had too many glitches and was susceptible to hacking. Hugo called them out on it, and the app flopped."

"Not because Hugo called him out on it then," Alayah muttered, and Derek glanced at her.

"Correct. It was destined to fail, but Marcus didn't want to hear that. He's no longer with Granite Intelligence, though."

"He could still carry a grudge," Efren said, leaning back in his seat.

"That's the reason I included him," Derek confirmed. "The other business is Forest Networks, which Spencer Williams owns. I'm behind the eight ball for this one because I don't know why he and Hugo hated each other. They run in the same circles and are close to the same age, but other than that, I don't know a lot about Spencer. When I asked Hugo, he refused to answer."

"It's a woman," Selina said without hesitation. "It's always a woman in these situations."

"That had never crossed my mind," Derek admitted, Selina's lips splitting into a grin.

"That's because you're a guy. Trust me on this one. It's a woman. We will find her."

"It's hard to believe that a guy like Hugo Victor had only two enemies," Cal said, leaning on a table. "Considering the business he was in, a person picks them up simply because they exist."

"That's accurate, but these three are the ones I remember being a real thorn in Hugo's side. I don't have access to the records that might give us more names, but something tells me maybe someone on your staff can bypass those pesky log-ins and passcodes to find them." Roman bit back a grin at his implication. "If I had to put my bets on one of these guys, it would be Josh. He's the one with the most to gain from Hugo's death," Derek said, tapping the name again.

"Explain," Cal said.

"With Hugo dead, the business will likely go into public trading. If that happens, it's a door for Josh to enter and slowly infiltrate the company again." A thought struck Derek, and he snapped his fingers, turning to write another name on the board. "This one almost escaped my memory. It may not be a big deal, but I'll mention it in the interest of transparency. John Lavelle owns Clover Industries. His company makes things like paper products and such, so not remotely the same as Black Marlin, but Curtis Clemons was his chief operating officer before Hugo wooed him away."

"People leave jobs all the time for better positions and greener pastures," Cal said.

"You're not wrong, but less than two months later, Salma Barker left Clover Industries and came to Black Marlin Technologies."

"That feels suspicious. Were they setting Hugo up?"

"We never saw it that way. Salma's husband accepted a job as a bigwig at an insurance company in Minneapolis. Salma reached out to Curtis since she knew he was working in town and asked about companies that might be hiring."

"Okay, then all you can say there is 'that's business,'" Zac said, swiveling in his seat. "You can't get upset because an employee finds a job with a competitor when they're forced to move."

"Exactly what Hugo told him, but John was hot about it and accused Hugo of purposely targeting him."

"How long ago was that?" Cal asked, and Derek counted back to when the board was set up. "About ten years ago? It was long before my time with the company or as Hugo's assistant. Of course, if you want a list of all the people who have ever had an issue with Black Marlin, it will be long. Hugo had a short fuse for mistakes, so plenty of people came and went in the company over the years."

"Sounds like the kind of guy who was hard to like," Mack said, and Derek shrugged.

"Not so much hard to like as hard to work for. When I first started working for him, he worked sunup to sundown. It took me a few years, but I taught him about work-life balance. He told me in the car on the way here that he was moving toward semi-retirement, which was another reason

I decided to turn in my resignation. If he was moving that direction, my job would become obsolete."

"It looks like someone wanted him in permanent retirement. I'll see if we can get a list of people with an ax to grind before the cops do," Cal said. "While that's being populated, we'll look closely at Josh and Marcus. Chances are that John was annoyed with him ten years ago, but is no longer in a murderous rage about losing a few employees. He doesn't have a compelling motive for murder, in my opinion."

"Agreed," Declan and Alayah said together, making everyone chuckle.

Cal glanced at his watch. "We're going to wrap this for tonight. I want everyone to get a hot meal and some sleep. We'll have our friends back at Secure Watch running some of this stuff down overnight. Let's meet for breakfast at 0700 hours."

Derek noticed the fatigue on everyone's faces as they packed up their laptops and headed out of the room. Guilt lanced through him for putting them through this until he remembered that Cal had a vested interest in finding Hugo's killer, too.

Chapter Sixteen

Once they were alone in the room with just Cal and Roman, Derek asked the question he really wanted the answer to. "Have you heard from Detective Henry?"

"Not today, but Ryland is running interference for us," Cal answered. "He's forcing them to go through him to get to either you or me. Henry has nothing on us besides the water bottle being in both of our hands. Alayah said that there was more than one?"

"I have four bottles that all look the same," Derek explained. "Hugo was superstitious about using this particular type when doing a presentation, but I never wanted to be caught with my pants down if it got lost, so I kept extras around. This time, I only brought one because I wasn't going to be here, and I didn't want him to know that there was more than one bottle."

"He didn't know?" Roman asked in surprise.

"That would be like telling your kid you have two of their favorite blankets and trade them out to wash one. No, he didn't know. I kept them at my house, other than the one in his office."

"No one else has access to them?" Cal asked.

"Anyone could access the one at the office," Derek said. "The extras would be more difficult to get to unless you knew they existed, but it was probably the worst-kept secret in the company. Hugo was the only one who didn't know about it."

"I can't say that helps you in any way," Roman said. "It would be better if you didn't keep the spares at home."

"You think someone switched the water bottle?" Derek asked, his brow furrowed.

"The antifreeze had to get in there some way, and it sure wasn't you," Alayah said.

"I assumed someone had tampered with it once it was onstage, but you're right. There would be little time to do anything to it when no one was looking or when video cameras weren't recording."

"Are the bottles still sold in stores?" Alayah asked.

"At just about every big-box store in the nation. It's not like they have a special logo or anything. He just liked how they fit in his hand and that the built-in straw made it easy for him to drink from it while wearing a microphone."

"And he uses the same one at every conference? Or at least one that always looked the same?" Cal asked, and Derek nodded. "That means his weakness was always on display."

"I hadn't thought of it that way, but yes. It was a sure bet that if Hugo was at a conference, that water bottle was close at hand. It wouldn't be difficult to purchase the same one."

"We need to look at Josh for this," Cal said to Roman. "We know he's in town, and he has the opportunity, means and motive."

"He was a rival for sure, but it's hard to get there with murder," Derek said, to which Cal shrugged.

"There are people in this world who will do anything to get ahead, and this guy sounds like the type. We'll dig deeper into his past. How far along are you with watching the security footage? I've sent all the streams to you."

"Not as far as I'd like," Alayah said. "But we had a lot coming at us today that prevented me from fully mapping everything. I got the camera feeds showing me dropping him off at the gas station and picking him back up again, as well as him inside the store. While that doesn't prove his innocence, it does prove that the recount we provided was accurate to time as well as his condition. After we eat, I plan to start mapping the security cameras here to track his movement through the convention center."

"Sleep first," Cal said, lowering an eyebrow at the woman. "You haven't had much in the last four days, and we can't afford mistakes. I would put one of the Secure Watch people on it, but you're more likely to catch him walking through places where his back is turned than they are. It's a first-thing-in-the-morning job. We can't put it off any longer. It's the only way to clear him."

"What about you?" Derek asked, watching the exchange.

"I've been in worse jams," Cal said with a shrug, as though that were the end of it.

"I'll be mapping Cal's movement, too, as well as the stagehands who touched the bottle," Alayah clarified.

Cal turned to her. "No need on that one. They've already been cleared. They never moved the water bottle. The video shows one of them lifting the bottle to shift the stand, and the other moved the bottle aside so he could set a piece of paper down."

"That just leaves my boss and the victim's assistant to clear. No pressure," Alayah said, biting her lip. "I'll have the maps done by morning with time stamps for both of you. If there are any dead zones in coverage anywhere, I'll also mark those so we can look for other cameras or images that might have caught you."

"Still a problem if there's crucial time missing. It wouldn't take but a few seconds to dump in antifreeze," Derek mused.

"You're not helping." Alayah's words were tight, and he bit back a resigned sigh.

"Call me when you have it ready," Cal said. "I don't care what time it is, but you need a few hours of rest before you do anything."

Alayah nodded, and Cal and Roman left, leaving them alone in the room. She turned to him. "I will find a way to clear you, Derek. I know you didn't do this."

When he smiled, he hoped it reflected all his sincerity and appreciation for her. "Knowing you have my back is what keeps me going right now, Alayah. It's nice to know someone cares."

When she smiled, he saw how true that was.

THE WIND WHISPERED across Alayah's face as she turned toward the lake. Stars twinkled above them, and for the first time in too long, silence reigned supreme. It was late, but she didn't care as she sat on the balcony of Derek's hotel room with a chicken sandwich in one hand and a glass of wine in the other. It was just what she needed to refresh her body and refocus her mind. If only she could refocus on her work and not on the man sitting beside her.

"Hugo sure knew how to book a hotel room," she said, leaning back in the chair packed with pillows to prop her up. He made a sound that turned her head. The smirk he wore as he chewed made her realize what she'd said. "Okay, *you* sure know how to book a hotel room."

He tipped his head in agreement as he sipped his beer.

"Hugo had very specific wants. Especially when he stayed in Duluth. I could get used to this view for the rest of my life."

"The option is yours now," she said with a shrug. "You don't have to go back to the city."

"True, but I do have to find work somewhere. I've decided not to worry about that until all of this is over. I can live in my cabin until December hits, so that's my fallback plan for now if need be."

"Were you raised in Minneapolis?" she asked, finishing her sandwich and setting her glass down on the table. The hotel restaurant had been accommodating, allowing her to order a kid's meal for ease in handling. She also couldn't eat a lot at one time due to her narrow chest. If her stomach became too full, it pressed up against her ribcage, making it uncomfortable and harder to breathe. For that reason, she'd learned to graze throughout the day and avoid large meals.

"Yes, in one of the suburbs, but the cabin is where I feel like I grew up. We spent a lot of time there with my grandparents in the summer," he said. "Then I went to college at the University of Minnesota and started my internship at Black Marlin, where I worked for many years before accepting the job as Hugo's assistant. I traveled extensively with Hugo, which was a definite perk of the job. We always attended the conference and then spent a few extra days sightseeing before returning."

"It sounds like Hugo enjoyed spending time with you. Not many bosses would do that."

He nodded, setting his beer down and peering out at the blackened lake. "Now that my exhaustive work blinders are gone, it's easy to see that's true. That was harder to see when I was exhausted while in the trenches. Some days, I felt more like a babysitter than an assistant. On those rare days that we hung out doing something other than work, that feeling disappeared. In hindsight, I can see that our relationship was multifaceted." She took his hand and kept hold of it in the silence. "We're always talking about me. What about you? Did you grow up in Minnesota?"

"Oh, no," she said with a shake of her head. "Pennsylvania. I'm Amish."

"Come again now?" he said, turning to her in surprise.

Her laughter broke the silence of the night. "Sorry, I should have said I was born into the Amish community. My parents were Old Order Amish from Lancaster. Ellis-Van Creveld Syndrome is typically found only in that population in the United States. When I was born, my parents were like…" She waved her hand at her throat and tossed her thumb over her shoulder.

"They left?" Her nod was short. "That's…wow."

"In their defense, their world was so much different than the one we live in, even when I was born thirty-two years ago. Suddenly, they were faced with a child who required extensive medical care, and they had no means to provide it. I could be bitter about it, but they gave me a fighting chance by doing the hardest thing they've ever done. Over half of babies born with my form of dwarfism don't make it to eighteen months. I'm probably only here because they were selfless when faced with overwhelming choices.

"I have a letter they wrote and asked to be sent with me wherever I was taken. My mother's pain was real as she scrawled her hopes and dreams for me on the paper. She was a mother and wanted what was best for me, but she knew she couldn't give me that.

"I was sent to Boston Children's Hospital and lived there for the first six months of my life. I required open heart surgery and pulmonary procedures." She held up her left hand.

"See this scar?" she asked, pointing to her palm below her pinkie finger, and he nodded. "That was from the removal of an extra finger. I had them on both hands and extra toes on both feet. To say I was a medically fragile and complex child was an understatement."

"I had no idea," he whispered, taking her hand again.

"Most don't. They see the overall picture and think, *Oh, she's a little person*. It's more complex than that. Do you know what I mean?" she asked, and he nodded. "I was also born without baby teeth or nails."

He lowered his brow and leaned in to inspect her hands, his eyes widening when he realized the truth. "Those are painted onto your skin. I never noticed."

"Most don't," she said with a shrug. "My nail technician uses a special paint. I can't do artificial nails because there isn't anything to stick them to."

"If you were born without baby teeth, what did you do until your adult ones came in?"

"I had temporary dentures as a child that worked okay, but weren't ideal. After consulting with a dentist, it was determined that I had sparse adult teeth as well, so those were pulled and I got a full set of implant dentures in high school."

"I'm sure all of that is just the tip of the iceberg of what you've been through," he whispered. "Did you live in medical foster care?"

"That's what one would expect, right? But no, I was extremely fortunate to have the best adoptive parents in the world. My mother was a nurse at Boston Children's Hospital. It didn't take her long to realize I had no visitors or family. I'd had no skin-to-skin contact with another human that wasn't painful, so she stepped in. She was a NICU nurse, but after her shift, she stayed the way a mom would. She came in on her days off and was there for the surgeries, setbacks and little victories.

"Soon, her husband, who was a surgeon there, started coming with her on the weekends to see me, and they applied for an emergency foster care license. There was no way she was letting me leave the hospital with anyone but her. In the end, they adopted me while I was still in the hospital, so when I came home, it was to stay. We moved to Pennsylvania when she took a different job, and we lived there until I was ten. Then, we moved to California when she was recruited for a management position in one of the children's hospitals. I attended college and worked in Silicon Valley for years. When they decided to move to Florida to retire, I also wanted a change, so I applied to Secure Watch. For the first time in my life, I moved thousands of miles away from the two people who had always taken care of me. It was a difficult adjustment at first, but now I love the independence. More than that, I love that they can enjoy their life without worrying about me."

"They love you, so they still worry about you," he said, and she nodded.

"True, but it's a healthier kind of worry now. They're both retired, so they do a lot of free care around the country in low-income clinics and such. I see them every few months, and I miss them between visits. They're thinking about moving to the Midwest. It turns out Florida isn't for them, but they also don't want to move back to a big city. They find their time in the Midwest working in rural communities invigorating, so they're exploring that now."

"We need more people like them in this world," he said, and she nodded vigorously.

"You're not kidding. I'll always be grateful for the sequence of events that brought them into my life. I can never have kids, but if I could, I would want to be just like her."

"You can't have kids?"

She inhaled deeply for a moment before responding. It was always hard for her to admit, even though she had known from a young age that she could never be a mother.

"Imagine this body growing a child and giving birth to it," she said, motioning at herself.

"I didn't think dwarfism precluded pregnancy, but maybe that just shows my ignorance."

"It depends on the dwarfism," she said with a shrug. "My kind of dwarfism is a hard and firm no. My truncal size alone excludes it, but my heart wouldn't handle the added fluid and requirements to sustain a pregnancy. I had a hysterectomy during one of my rib surgeries when I was sixteen."

"That had to have been a tough decision," he said, and she could tell he was trying to assimilate what she was telling him, but she was sure he hadn't yet considered what it meant for his life if they became involved. He would. They always did.

"It was an easy decision for me, but much harder to convince a doctor to do it. I went to a counselor who agreed I was aware of the implications of having my uterus removed. I was trying to prevent an emergency situation if I were to become pregnant. In my opinion, there was no reason to keep it if I could never use it."

"That's fair," he answered. "I still wish you hadn't dealt with so much, so young." After a check of his watch, he sighed. "It's almost eleven. We'd better get that sleep that Cal talked about so we can get back to clearing my name and finding Hugo's killer. Once we've done that, I have plans to make, big and small," he said as he stood and helped her down off the chair.

As they got ready for bed, his words ran through her mind. He had plans to make, big and small, but she was sure as soon as the penny dropped, the small ones would fall by the wayside. She always did.

Chapter Seventeen

After flopping onto his back, Derek couldn't deny he was a coward. Instead of asking Alayah to come to bed with him, he'd wished her a good night, walked to his room and shut the door. After she'd opened her heart and shared her past pain with him, he'd treated her as though she didn't matter. When the truth was, she had become the only thing that mattered to him. When he took Alayah's hand, she grounded him in this whirlwind that his life had become.

He hadn't realized the extent of her syndrome or the situations she's faced since birth. Knowing what she lives with on a day-to-day basis only solidified his respect for her in both life and work. It also helped him understand why she was so all-in with helping him. She knew what it was like to be the underdog and didn't want an injustice to occur on her watch. With a groan, he rolled over and checked the clock. It was only 1:30 a.m. It was going to be a long night.

There was a slight scrape on the wooden floor outside his door, so he climbed from the bed and quietly cracked the door to check on her. He shouldn't have been surprised to see her sitting at the computer desk, but he still was. When he'd said good-night two hours ago, her eyelids were drooping as she'd climbed onto the sofa bed. Deciding he should encourage her to go back to sleep, he left his room and padded toward her in his bare feet.

"Alayah? What are you doing awake?"

"I couldn't sleep, so I decided to be productive," she said. "I started mapping Cal's route of running the torch."

Derek couldn't hide his amusement as he pulled up a chair to sit beside her. "You really should be sleeping."

"So should you," she answered without taking her eyes off her work. "But here you are."

His smile was wide as she leaned in to watch the multiple screens that played videos from different camera angles. "This looks like tedious work."

"The worst," she agreed. "But imperative when getting the timeline right. If I can find the last ten-second span of time that's missing, I've got Cal cleared."

"Really?" he asked in surprise, and she nodded.

"We know he went from the conference room to the stage without stopping, but there's one stretch that doesn't appear to have a camera."

"And ten seconds is plenty long enough to slip poison in a bottle or trade one out."

Her nod appeared to be her answer as she clicked her mouse, the different camera angles enlarging and shrinking as she searched for her boss. "As soon as I finish this, I'll start on your journey. I've already noted several places where I've seen you without the water bottle, so I can work back from there."

"Alayah, you really do need sleep."

"What I really need is for people to stop telling me what I need. The only person who knows that is me."

Rather than say anything, he stayed silent as she continued to watch the feeds until she clicked to pause them.

"I'm sorry. That was rude. It's been a long week with a

lot of work, but none more important than this. I can't do a lot, but I can clear you and Cal of this murder charge hanging over your heads. Once that's done, I'll sleep for hours."

Understanding how stressed she was and that he was partly to blame, he massaged her neck while she clicked the mouse. "I apologize for pushing. You know what you need, and I'll do whatever I can to help. You can run circles around me in the cyberworld, though, so there's not much I can do."

"Keep doing what you're doing," she answered. "I'll take a neck massage all day long after spending hours at the keyboard." Before he could say anything, she clicked once on the mouse and did a fist pump. "Gotcha!"

"What did I miss?" he asked as she started writing on a notepad beside her.

Her finger moved to the screen on her left. "Watch." Then she clicked the mouse and started the video feed. A large group of people was milling around in front of the conference room doors. They were obviously waiting for the doors to open so they could find their seats.

"I don't see anything."

"Neither did I the first three times I watched it, but I'll slow it down." After a couple of clicks, the video slowed, and she pointed to the right side of the screen.

"It's Cal!" he exclaimed when he finally noticed the only person moving through the crowd and not just standing around. "He was easy to miss since he walked behind everybody to get to the other hallway."

"Exactly," she said with a relieved sigh as she leaned back in the chair. "He's cleared. There isn't one second of his walk from the conference room to backstage that's not accounted for. Thank God," she said, her shoulders drooping under his hands. "Once I call him, I'll need to package this up and email it."

"Maybe you should hold off on that. It's late," he said logically, stopping her from dialing.

When she lowered her brow at him, he had to bite back a laugh. "Trust me, he'll want to know about this."

Derek released her hand, and she called while he wandered to the kitchenette. He made each of them a cup of coffee, knowing that her success in clearing Cal would drive her to keep going until she cleared him as well. He'd do whatever he could to support her in that. When he returned to the desk, he set the coffee down as she lowered her phone.

"Coffee with two sugars and one cream," he said, sitting as she stuck a jump drive into her computer.

"You know how I like my coffee?" she asked in surprise.

"I'm observant," he said with a shrug. "What did Cal say?"

"He had plenty to say about me not following his orders until I reminded him that I didn't sign up for the army when I joined Secure Watch." Derek bit his lip to keep from laughing. She did that to him often. "That said, he was understandably relieved that we can send this information to Detective Henry tomorrow to clear him." While she talked, she was zipping files inside a folder and transferring them to the flash drive. "He wants a hard copy on Henry's desk in the morning, so he's calling a squad over to pick it up. Would you run this jump drive down to him while I keep working?"

"Wouldn't it be easier to email it?"

"Sure," she agreed. "And I did email it to Cal, but this is an encrypted copy that only Henry can open with the code inside the sealed envelope." After she dropped the jump drive and a piece of paper into the envelope, she sealed it and handed it to him. "Cal said he'd meet you in the lobby to wait for the police. I'm going to re-spool everything and start on the task of clearing you."

"Maybe we should just wait on this," he said, slipping his shoes on as he held up the envelope. "Won't we have to do the same thing with mine when you clear me?"

"Confidence looks good on you, Mr. Benjamin."

"All my confidence is in you, sweetheart," he assured her as he pulled on a sweatshirt.

"No pressure, right?" she teased. "Take that one now. It's important to get Cal cleared in case he needs to leave to attend to business at home. It could be tomorrow before I can finish yours."

"You got it." He walked over and kissed her gently on the lips. "For the record, I don't know what I did to deserve your help, but I promise not to let you down."

Before she could say anything, he left the room, knowing the winds of change were in his favor.

"CAL," DEREK CALLED when he got to the lobby. "I've got your get-out-of-jail-free card."

"Henry is on his way," Cal answered, refusing to take the envelope.

"Alayah said a squad was coming to get it."

"That was the plan," he said. "But he wants to see the evidence himself, and then he'll take the official copy back with him."

"Kind of late for a detective to be working, isn't it?" Derek asked as they waited by the main entrance.

"Maybe in the big city, but this is Duluth, and a huge tech bro died on their watch. I would imagine no one is sleeping until they find his killer. Especially since the clock is ticking as the conference winds down."

"Did you watch the footage?" Derek asked, leaning against the wall.

"On my phone in the elevator, and I've got it ready to go on a computer in the conference room once he gets here. Our girl did it. There isn't a second missing from the sequence. She's the best at that kind of digital tracking. That's why I gave her the job."

"Couldn't be happier you're free of the suspicion," Derek said with total sincerity. "The last thing I wanted was for any of you to get jammed up with this. You were just doing your job."

"So were you, and Alayah will prove it. Trust the process."

"That's easy to do when you trust the person who holds your future in her hands. If she isn't asleep by the time I return to the room, I'll have to pry her fingers off the keyboard and force her to bed."

"Good luck with that," he said, the words laced with sarcasm. "She's like a dog with a bone when something eludes her. She won't sleep until she finishes the job she was assigned. Then she might take five before asking for her next assignment. I kind of love that about her, even though Mina has to continually force her out of the control room after her shift."

"I've known her for two days, but that's easy to believe. She's very much a team player, and I'm extremely grateful to her and the entire team for coming to my defense."

Cal turned away from the door and stepped up to him, a little too close, in Derek's opinion, but there was nowhere for him to go when pinned against the wall. The man before him wore an expression that said things were about to get real. He stood his ground and waited for Cal to speak.

"Don't think I've forgotten what you did to her. I haven't. While I understand that you were dazed and confused, the choices you made forced her into making choices she otherwise wouldn't have, and she got hurt because of it. Fair warning—that was your only get-out-of-jail-free card. If you so much as harm one hair on her head, you will not be so lucky the second time around. Are we clear?"

"Crystal," he said in a tone that was confident in light of Cal's posture. "The last thing I want is to hurt Alayah. I'll beat myself up for the rest of my life that I put her in the position she was in with those guys. Trust me on that one."

Cal took a step back and gave him one last side-eye. "I do, which is the only reason you've gotten within ten feet of her since then. Don't make me regret it."

"Wouldn't cross my mind," Derek promised as a car pulled up and Detective Henry climbed out.

"Gentleman," he said when he approached. "This better be the real deal."

"It is," they said in unison, but the detective didn't even crack a smile.

Derek handed over the envelope to the detective. "That is an official, encrypted copy of the proof. The instructions are inside. With that, I shall return to my room."

"Stick with us," Henry said as Cal motioned them toward the conference room. "I may have questions for you after I watch this."

With a resigned nod, he followed the other men to the conference room. There was no reason he needed to stay, but he also didn't want to look combative at 2:30 in the morning. He could spare another ten minutes since Alayah had her head buried in the computer anyway.

"My operative was able to track every second from the time I took possession of the bottle until I left it onstage, as well as where I went from there until the speech started," Cal explained, starting the video after handing him a print-out of the time stamps.

The man worked fast. Then again, Derek probably would, too, if it was a matter of not going to jail for a murder you didn't commit. He sent up another silent prayer that Alayah was getting closer to proving that he wasn't responsible. Something about being accused of a crime made you question whether you somehow did it and blocked it out. Derek knew how that sounded, but he had run the scenario through his head hundreds of times over the last day just to double-check that it remained the same each time. When he'd handed that bottle over to Cal, it had been free of antifreeze, and he'd stand by that until the day he died. He just had to hope he could find a way to prove it.

Chapter Eighteen

"Come on, come on," Alayah chanted as she rode the elevator down to the first floor. She had to find Derek and Cal. She'd been trying to text them, but when they didn't respond, she'd grabbed her walker and headed down to find them.

She had lost track of time after Derek left, and when she'd looked up again, over thirty minutes had passed. Maybe he was just having a drink with Cal, but it was weird that they weren't responding to her texts. Especially since she had news they would want. The doors to the elevator slid open and she hurried out, looking left and right for any sign of them, but the hotel lobby was empty other than the receptionist at the desk. She noticed the clock and realized the bar was closed, so they weren't having a drink unless they were in Cal's room. Unsure what to do, she worried her lower lip between her teeth for a few minutes before she walked to the reservations desk.

"Have you seen a couple of guys down here in the last hour or so?" Alayah asked the woman. "They were waiting for the police to arrive."

"Oh, they're in the conference room," she said, pointing to the left, where Alayah finally noticed the door was ajar a bit.

"Thank you," she said with a smile before she hurried toward the room. They must have decided to go over the footage together before parting ways for the night. Cal likely had questions for Derek, and knowing Cal, a few choice words about her as well. Everyone at Secure Inc. was known to be overly protective of her, which she appreciated, but it was also difficult to navigate when she was a fully grown adult and capable of making her own decisions.

"You're under arrest for the murder of Hugo Victor," a man said as she pushed the door open. Detective Henry was slapping cuffs on Derek's wrists.

"Stop that!" she exclaimed, nearly falling when her walker wheel got stuck on the door. She abandoned it and limped toward them, anger and fear making her legs tremble. "He didn't kill Hugo Victor!"

"Alayah, keep your voice down," Cal said as he approached and grasped her arm to keep her from falling.

"I'll do no such thing!" she said, shaking her arm free. "What on earth is happening right now?"

"For your information," Henry said, snapping the cuffs. "Mr. Benjamin is being detained for the murder of Hugo Victor. With your boss cleared of the murder, it leaves me no choice but to arrest his assistant, as he was the only other person who had access to the bottle."

"That's not true," she said, shaking an envelope in her hand. "I can prove it."

Cal helped her to the table to sit before he knelt before her. "You have proof?"

She nodded and motioned for Henry and Derek to come over. She noticed that Henry had left the cuffs on Derek but hadn't started Mirandizing him, so she'd take it for now. "This was the official copy for the police, but since you're here and can see I'm not tampering with it, can I open it?"

Henry nodded for her to proceed, so she opened the drive and inserted it, then decrypted the files.

"I'm not sure how this will prove he didn't poison his boss," Henry said. "He brought the water bottle with them."

"Watch," Alayah said, starting the video, and everyone leaned in to see it better. She had slowed it down so she could speak as it played. "Here, you see Derek take the water bottle from Hugo, who had just taken a drink from it."

"The antifreeze could have already been in it," Henry said defiantly.

"He keeled over on stage quickly after drinking about half of the new bottle. It makes sense that if the antifreeze was in the bottle he just drank from, he would have died much sooner than he did, taking into account how quickly he died after drinking from the one on stage," Cal reasoned.

"To Cal's point," Alayah said, starting the tape again, "Derek takes the bottle to the water fountain, rinsing it out." She waited for it to play, and they watched as he walked to a vending machine and bought a bottle of the vitamin water Hugo liked. "He dumps the water from the vending machine into Hugo's bottle and screws on the lid."

"That raises two questions," Henry said. "Why didn't you bring his favorite water with you, and why dump it in another bottle when it's already in one?"

"I did bring a bottle of it with me," Derek explained. "Hugo drank it all on the way here. I can't prove it, but Hugo filled the bottle before we left, not me. Since it's a popular brand, I wasn't worried about not being able to get it, so I just grabbed a bottle from the machine. Hugo preferred his water bottle with a straw because it made it easier to drink when he had his head microphone on."

Alayah hit Play again before Henry could interrupt with more questions. She wanted those handcuffs off Derek.

"We can follow him all the way to the room where I was looking for coffee," she says, pointing herself out when the camera angle changed to inside the room. "We talk for a minute, and then I walk out. You see Derek standing there looking around the room, not messing with the bottle, until Cal walks in." She stopped talking as the tape continued to play. Cal and Derek shook hands and joked before Derek handed him the water bottle. Just to be on the safe side, she let it play until Cal walked out of the room with it, and then she stopped it. "As you can see. He had no time to put the antifreeze in the bottle, and it couldn't have been there to begin with because he rinsed the bottle out before refilling it."

Henry was silent, tension radiating from him as he stared at the screen. "It didn't just magically grow in the water bottle."

"That's correct," she said, holding up her finger and clicking on a different file. "I thought the same thing, so I went back to the feeds after Cal set the bottle down and after the stagehands were cleared. Look."

With a click of the mouse, the static feed of the stage played for about fifteen seconds before the screen went black. It stayed that way for almost a minute before the feed returned.

"What the hell?" Cal asked, leaning in. "Play that again."

After rewinding and playing it again, he stood and shook his head. "That's weird. I didn't see that the first time we watched the footage."

"You wouldn't have," she said with a smug smile. "Someone had planted a Trojan horse in the coding that looped the video for the minute it was actually out. No one would ever know the difference since it was just a static video of the empty stage. The only reason I found it was that I'd magnified the image on the water bottle and thought I saw it jump. The same thing happened every time I rewound it, but it wasn't noticeable when I zoomed out. That's when I dug into the video's coding and found it."

"And that's why we pay you the big bucks," Cal said with a satisfied smile. "Well done, Miss Heath."

Derek let out a sigh and his smile told her how grateful he was. "Thank God for Alayah."

"This was a fun show and all," Henry said, "but it doesn't clear Mr. Benjamin. His literal job is coding. He could easily have done this with very little trouble."

"Had he been here," Alayah said. "I saved the best for last." With a flourish, she clicked on the final video in the file and let it play. It showed Derek leaving the convention center just minutes after Cal set the bottle on stage and long before the feed was cut. He reappeared in the parking lot, removed his jacket and climbed in his car, then pulled out. The timestamps on the videos showed that the stage feed went black at the same time Derek was driving away.

The room was silent as they waited for Detective Henry to speak. He stood staring at the monitor, his jaw ticking to the beat of his case falling apart, and she hung her hopes on that final time stamp. Finally, he walked over to Derek and unlocked the cuffs. She was sure her relieved sigh was heard around the world.

"In light of this, I have some more work to do to confirm what was found. However, as of right now, the only person I can clear with any certainty is Mr. Newfellow. He may leave town. You may not. Do you understand?"

"Crystal clear," Derek said, rubbing at his shoulder. "We both want the same thing, Detective Henry. To see

Hugo's killer behind bars. I assure you that isn't me. I will do whatever you ask of me until you figure out who killed my friend."

Detective Henry didn't appear impressed by Derek's impassioned plea, instead pointing at her. "I need both of those drives, so our digital recovery team can follow the same trail to see if they come to the same conclusion. If anything deviates from what you just showed me, you'll find yourself behind bars for tampering with evidence."

"I stand behind my work," she assured him, disengaging the jump drive and putting it back in the envelope, then handing both to him. "There will be no discrepancies. If your team has any questions, you know how to reach me." Maybe it was the late hour, or maybe she was tired of feeling small around men like him, but there wasn't so much as a hint of fear in her voice when she spoke.

"I'll show you out," Cal said, motioning for the detective to follow him. He turned back to them. "Sleep. I don't want to see you before nine a.m. tomorrow. Preferably ten."

The moment they were gone, Derek knelt before her and pulled her into his arms. "You are a rock star with impeccable timing."

"Unless you're Detective Henry, then I'm a killjoy," she said, loving how his laughter rumbled through her. "I knew you didn't do it, so it was just a matter of finding the proof."

He trailed a finger down her cheek. "I don't know how I got so lucky to meet you in this room just a few days ago, but I'll thank the universe for that until the day I die. What do you say we go get some of that sleep everyone keeps talking about?"

Once he had retrieved her walker from the doorway, she followed him to the elevator. When they stepped on, and it lifted them toward the reward of her hard work, she wondered if that was sleep or something else entirely. While part of her wanted sleep, the other yearned to be held and loved, even for just one night.

Chapter Nineteen

Sleep wouldn't come for Alayah. When they'd returned to the room, Derek had wished her a good night and disappeared into the bedroom. She'd be lying to herself if she didn't notice the way he'd hesitated at the door when he'd said good-night. Almost like he was hoping she'd say something. The request to share his bed had been on the tip of her tongue, but she couldn't force the words passed her lips.

"Alayah?" His voice filled the darkness, and she jumped with a squeal, throwing a hand to her heart. "I didn't mean to scare you, but you've been flopping around like a fish out here. I was worried something was wrong."

"Can't sleep," she said, sitting up to rub her face. "Even though I'm beyond exhausted. That happens sometimes when I'm working on a big case. I know Cal is worried my ankle won't heal if I don't get enough rest, but it's fine. It only gives me an occasional twinge if I step on it wrong. I probably won't even need the walker by tomorrow."

"You'll use the walker," he said firmly. "At least for long distances around the hotel. You don't want to set your recovery back by overdoing it, right?"

"Yes, Selina," she said with a smirk that he probably couldn't see. "Sorry to have disturbed you. I'll try to keep it down out here."

He sat next to her on the sofa bed and took her hand. "I have a better idea. Why don't we share my bed? This one can't be all that comfortable."

Her laughter was more nervous than amused when it fell from her lips. "I've slept on better mattresses, and it's sweet of you to offer, but you shouldn't have to share. I'd need a stepstool to get up on that bed anyway."

"If I didn't want to share, I wouldn't have offered," he said, his brow furrowed. "Truthfully, when I said good-night, what I really wanted was you in my bed to hold. I'm not asking for more than that, Alayah. Just the opportunity to hold you and help you get some rest."

With her heart pounding, she pushed herself up and met his gaze. "As much as I've enjoyed our time together, a murder charge hanging over your head notwithstanding, there's so much about me that you don't know. None of that information is any easier than what I've already told you."

"And you think that means you don't deserve to be loved or to find happiness?"

"Maybe? I don't know. I'm tired." She did know and she could explain it, but she also didn't want to hurt him by implying that what he thought he was feeling tonight might be completely different come the morning light. He probably wouldn't like her putting words in his mouth, even if she knew they were true.

"Which brings us back to where we were a few minutes ago. Is it okay if I carry you? I don't want to hurt you."

Her head tipped in curiosity. "I can walk, Derek."

"Maybe, but you need help getting up on the bed, so why not take a ride?"

Heat rose on her cheeks at the thought of being in his arms. When she ducked her head, it was partly to hide her reaction and partly from embarrassment that she couldn't get on the bed without his help. "It's fine as long as you don't expect me to wrap my arms around your neck." She held up her arms and waved them.

Gently, he grasped her hands and lowered them to his lap. "I know what you're doing, Alayah, and I understand. It's hard for you to be intimate without feeling vulnerable, right?"

She lifted her head and nodded. What she saw on his handsome face was eagerness to be what she needed him to be and she wished for the millionth time in her life that she had been born differently. Then she remembered her life would be completely different had she been born without the syndrome. The family she had at Secure Inc. wouldn't exist, and she wouldn't have met Derek. Though they'd go their separate ways, she was still blessed to have known him.

"I want you to understand that I respect you and you have full control over what happens from here forward. If you'd rather I carry your stepstool into the bedroom instead of you, I'm happy to do that if it makes you feel more comfortable and in control."

His offer told her he understood her fears. Maybe it was time to help him understand her desires. "I'd love a ride to bed. Thank you."

Tenderly, he scooped her up into his chest and cradled her there as he carried her to the bedroom. The bed was king-sized and piled high with pillows. "I might get lost in this bed."

"Unlikely," he said, lowering her to the mattress to rest up against the pillows. "Since you'll be in my arms the entire night, I'll keep you safe. What's the best way for you to sleep? I feel like you don't sleep on your back to avoid compression on your chest."

Her sharp glance at him revealed his expressionless face as he waited for her to answer. "No one has ever listened to what I say closely enough to come to a conclusion like that, Derek."

"It's not hard to listen to someone you care about, Alayah."

"Most don't," she answered with a shrug. "It means the entire world to me that you did, though. It's a simple thing to you, but for me, it's..." She made the mind-blown motion with her hands. He took her hand and rubbed his thumb over her knuckles while he waited patiently for her to finish her thought. Heat spiraled through her at his touch, so she cleared her throat to avoid sounding needy. "You're right. Usually, I sleep elevated, almost sitting up. If I can't do that, then I sleep on my side with pillows behind me so I don't fall backward."

"Easy enough," he said, propping the pillows along the headboard until there was a ramp of sorts and then leaning into them, pulling her back in the process. Once he had the covers over them, he snugged her into his side with her head on his shoulder. "A perfect fit." His words were a whisper as he leaned down and brushed his lips across hers in a tender kiss of understanding. "Are you comfortable?"

She nodded, fighting back tears at just how understanding he was and at how perfectly she fit against him. Her eyelids drooped as he rubbed her shoulder, her body refusing to stay awake a moment longer. As she drifted off to sleep, she heard him whisper, "I would be a lucky man to get to hold you like this forever, Alayah Heath."

A sigh of happiness escaped her lips as she fell into dreamland.

THE NEXT TIME she woke, the room was starting to brighten, which meant a new day had arrived, and she could only imagine what would come of it. She should be cataloging everything she had left to do, but now that she'd cleared Cal and Derek, her brain wanted to take a break from all the thinking. It wanted to enjoy being in a warm pair of arms as they cuddled together under the blankets. Since they had hours until their team meeting, she was going to do exactly that. Once she made a trip to the bathroom, that is. As much as she hated to get up and risk waking Derek, she had no choice.

In sleep, he'd loosened his arms, and she was able to slide out of them and to the edge of the bed without waking him. Getting off the bed was another matter, but she managed by sliding over the edge on her belly until her feet touched the floor. Thankfully, her ankle no longer hurt. She would take that as a solid win. She'd still protect it, but if she could avoid using the walker all day, that would be helpful.

Derek seemed to think her reluctance to use the walker stemmed only from embarrassment, but it was also about the pain in her shoulders, elbows and hands from using it all day. That was one of the reasons she'd worked so hard in physical therapy over the years. She didn't want to use it any more than necessary. It was fine when she was hurt, but she preferred getting around under her own volition the rest of the time. Besides, her physical therapist had emphasized the importance of keeping her muscles strong, so she had a set of weights that she lifted at home. While she couldn't use most gym equipment, she also had a program for lower leg exercises that kept her limber and strong. Even if it didn't look that way to the average person.

After using the restroom and brushing her teeth, she snuck a look at the clock on the way past to see it was almost 6:00 a.m. They could spend at least another two hours in bed before they had to think about getting up, and she planned to enjoy every second of it. They'd only been asleep for about three hours, but she felt rested and ready to go for the day. That was likely because her body was used to short stints of sleep when working time-sensitive jobs at Secure Watch. Once the job was finished, she'd pass out and sleep for twelve or sixteen hours and then be ready to start all over again. She'd learned over the years that many coders and cybersecurity people had sleep issues. Their brains didn't want to shut down when struggling with a complex problem that needed fixing. Especially if the case involved someone's personal or business safety. She often worried that stepping away for a few hours to rest could be the reason a case fell apart. Last night, she'd needed sleep and though the job wasn't over, at least she'd be able to attack it today with renewed vigor.

"Hey," Derek said, making her jump as she approached the bedroom door. "Sorry, I didn't mean to scare you. I was using the other bathroom."

"I didn't mean to wake you," she said with a frown, but he shook his head and motioned her to the bed.

"Don't apologize. We can snuggle back together for a few hours since Cal said we had until nine, right?"

"At the earliest," she agreed as he helped her back onto the bed with a gentle lift from her hips. "But I want to be there when he briefs the team, so we should aim for nine."

"When I woke up, it took my brain a few seconds to catch up to what happened last night," he admitted, pulling her into him again. "It took me some time to remember that this beautiful and brilliant woman I'd held all night long had managed to give me my future back with her dogged determination. Maybe I'm not completely out of the woods yet, but now we have breathing room to figure out who really killed Hugo."

She raised her hand to stroke his jaw, a bit of scruff tickling her fingers. "We'll figure it out. That's what we do at Secure Watch. We protect and serve, just in a different way than Detective Henry."

"He's a total blowhard," he said, laughing even harder when she joined him with her hee-haw laugh.

"Cybersecurity is the kind of job where you rarely get to see interactions like last night, but nothing was more satisfying than seeing his face when he realized his entire case had fallen apart."

"It was a moment of relief for me," he said, leaning toward her. She wound her fingers into his hair, bringing his lips to hers in a kiss that left her dizzy with anticipation and need. Derek broke the lip lock to trail his lips down her neck to her collarbone.

"What are you doing?" she asked as he moved her sleep shirt aside to kiss her shoulder.

"Kissing you," he whispered. "Isn't it obvious?"

She pulled her shirt back over her shoulder. "Trust me, you don't want to take those kisses any further."

When he sat up, it was easy to read the confusion in his eyes. "Because?"

"Because of so many reasons, Derek. You can't understand, so I won't bother to explain it," she said, leaning back against the pillows.

"Saying you won't bother to explain it because I can't understand is insulting, Alayah. Saying that you don't know how to explain it leaves room for an open discussion."

Her frown deepened when she glanced up into his face, his expression honest and caring. "I'm sorry. It's not that you can't understand it. It's that I can't explain it."

"Or maybe it's that you can't explain how I could feel differently about your body than you do?" Her nod was her only answer. "It would be easy to fall back on the old saying of beauty is in the eye of the beholder here, right?" She nodded again with a shrug. "And while that's true, I suspect it goes deeper than that for you. This is about the bigger picture. It's about everything you've internalized regarding the things you were told were wrong with you, even though there's nothing wrong with you."

"There's plenty wrong with me, Derek," she said with a derisive laugh. "From my strangely shaped torso to the scars crisscrossing it, not to mention my protruding forehead and impossibly short arms and legs."

"And you can feel that way if you want to," he agreed. "But I want you to consider my version of that story. It's different, that's for sure, but maybe it's a kinder way to treat yourself. I haven't seen the scars, but what I have seen paints a much different picture of who you are."

"You're going to say my skills as a cybersecurity agent and my childlike innocence, right?" she asked, trying to keep the sarcasm at bay but fearing it slipped in anyway.

His mouth opened to respond, but then he closed it again and held up his finger. "I think it's time for show rather than tell," he said as he lowered himself to the bed and laid his lips on hers.

"Derek," she whispered as he kissed his way down her arm. "What are you doing?"

"Kissing you," he answered, kissing the tip of every finger. When he was finished, he brought his lips back to hers for another tangle of tongues that left them both breathing heavily.

She was about to beg him to keep going when a sound from the other room stopped her. "That's my phone."

"Leave it," he whispered, dropping his head to place a kiss on her chest. "They'll call back."

When the ringing stopped, she relaxed into the mattress as he lifted her shirt just a hair to feather his lips across her navel, drawing a quick breath from her lips before heat pooled low in her belly. Suddenly, the sound of a trumpet filled the room.

"Is that 'Reveille'?" he asked, lifting his head.

"Cal was an army guy," she said with a smirk before she realized what it meant. "That's an all-call alert! Quick, grab my phone."

Derek darted from the room and was back in record time, holding out her Secure Watch phone. Before she had it to her ear, she answered. The voice on the other end was calm, but it did nothing to quell the tremor of anxiety that went through her at his explanation.

"We'll come to your room." She paused as he continued speaking, then nodded. "Heard and understood. See you in ten."

Whatever look was on her face had him turning on the bedside lamp. "Something happened."

"You could say that," she agreed, swallowing down the bile threatening to erupt. "Josh Hunt was just found floating face down in Lake Superior."

Chapter Twenty

When Cal opened the door to his room a mere ten minutes later, the rest of the team was already gathered. Derek could still taste Alayah's sweetness on his lips and wanted nothing more than to be back in bed with her, pretending that the outside world didn't exist. It couldn't be a coincidence that Josh and Hugo died at the same conference. Someone was killing tech giants, and he wanted to know who and why.

"Fill us in," Alayah said as she sat next to Selina and patted the chair beside her. He slipped into the seat and rested his hand on her knee. When he touched her, his center calmed, and he could concentrate on what Cal had to say.

"I got a call from Detective Henry about thirty minutes ago that Josh Hunt was found floating in the Superior Harbor by a passerby. As we are security for the conference, he had to notify me that another speaker was killed."

"Is he sure the guy didn't just fall in? Maybe he was drunk or something?" Efren asked from the other side of the room.

"While he wouldn't share how Josh was killed, he assured me it was undoubtedly murder," Cal answered.

"Josh was an attendee and guest speaker, but he wasn't staying here," Derek said. "At this hotel, I mean."

"He wasn't," Cal agreed, walking to the whiteboard he'd

propped up against the television. He wrote "The Suites" in black. "He was staying at this hotel a few blocks away. When I spoke to him yesterday, he said he preferred hotels directly on the water when he was in Duluth."

"Okay, but why would they find him all the way in Superior and not just outside his hotel room door? If he was found in Superior, the trip was purposeful. He had to drive across the bridge to get to that harbor. There had to be a reason," Efren deduced.

Cal nodded. "That was mine and Detective Henry's thought, too. Had he just fallen into the water outside the hotel or at Park Point, you could assume he was drunk or slipped. Driving all the way to Superior feels purposeful."

"Maybe he went to one of the restaurants over there?" Eric suggested with a shrug. "Or he had a hookup planned at a hotel where no one knew him?"

"According to the information I received from the detective, which was reluctantly, I might add, there's video footage of Josh leaving his room at 0300 hours."

"Bars are closed by three a.m. around here," Roman said, and Cal nodded before he started writing again.

"Right, so he leaves Duluth at 0300 hours, and assuming he drove directly to Superior, where they found his car, that's a ten- to fifteen-minute drive, probably ten when the roads are relatively empty. He arrives at the marina, or at least that's where they found his car, and does what? It's 0315 or 0330 at the latest. Maybe he was hooking up with someone on one of the docked boats? That's a possibility."

"Do we have any footage from the marina to show his arrival and what he did while there?" Zac asked.

"Not yet, but it's supposedly coming. I doubt we'll be privy to it once they have it."

Alayah's laughter lifted Derek's lips. "Like that's ever stopped us before."

Cal pointed at her, his metal-and-plastic fingers making a telltale clicking sound in the room. "And it won't stop us this time, but my guess is, whatever the footage shows, it won't be his death. Maybe we'll get lucky, and it will show him entering a boat or meeting someone, but if it was anything more than an innocent hookup, there's no way he'd meet someone in an area with cameras."

"That's the odd part," Alayah agreed. "Why would he park his car somewhere with security cameras if he wasn't going to meet them there?"

"Proof of life at the time he parked," Selina answered, and everyone swiveled to her. "Think about it. If this was something other than a hookup on a houseboat and he didn't return to his car, it would be found as soon as the marina opened, and people would start asking questions."

"Like someone took him hostage?" Derek asked, and she nodded with a shrug.

"That or he knew the meeting could result in his death. There's no way to know what he was thinking when he parked there."

"Well, we know that whatever he was doing, he didn't want anyone to know," Cal added. "He didn't leave a note, at least on paper. The police are looking at his electronic footprint."

"So that brings me back to a hookup," Alayah said. "Working on that theory, the question is, how did he end up in the water? Obviously, if the detective said he was murdered, it likely wasn't by drowning. He had to have been killed before he went into the water. Why would a hookup end in death?"

"Unless he was lured there on the pretense of a hookup, but it was a setup," Derek said, and Cal clapped once.

"Yes! Now that makes more sense," he agreed, writing *setup* with a question mark on the board before writing *who* and *why*. "Our job is to answer these questions," he said, tapping the board.

"Isn't that the cops' job?" Derek asked.

"Technically," Cal said. "But we don't have to work around the bureaucracy that they do. Since the conference has officially been canceled, but we're all suspects, we may as well focus on clearing everyone to extract ourselves from this mess."

"We're all suspects?" Alayah asked. "Let me guess. Detective Henry told you that."

"But who else?" Cal asked, tongue in cheek. "Actually, the only ones who are cleared would be me, you and Derek since we were meeting with him at the time Josh left his hotel."

Alayah did the math in her head. "We returned to the room about 0330 hours. If they move his time of death to even thirty minutes later, then we're still suspects. We won't know for sure until the autopsy is complete. That said, the only person with a reason to meet up with Josh would be Derek."

"Gee, just when I think I'm in the clear," he muttered.

"But you were with me all night," Alayah reminded him. "Uh, I mean, we were in the same room, so I'm his alibi," she clarified, but he would be lying if he said he didn't see the smirk on Selina's face.

"And we will need your skills to prove that alibi to the police. While it's true Josh was not my favorite person, I had no reason to meet up with him at that time of the morning."

"How do you want to break this down, boss?" Roman asked, leaning forward. "Our security services are no longer needed, which frees us up. Do you want us to head back to Secure Inc.?"

"You can't," he answered, leaning on a table. "Not until you've all been cleared. I want Zac and Declan to focus on using the hotel footage to clear everyone on the team. Text Zac the time you went to your room, if you left it at any point after that, where you went, and when you returned." He turned to Zac and Declan. "Clear the security team first." Zac nodded, so Cal continued. "While you're waiting, start packing up the equipment. I want to send everyone out of here in waves to ensure we have enough vehicles left here to get everyone home."

"What do you want me to do?" Alayah asked, and he held up his finger to her, which signaled to Derek that he wanted to discuss that in private.

"Roman, check in with Mina and see if she can get us that video footage from the marina. Have her send it to Alayah once she has it."

"If she has it," Roman said, pulling his phone out.

Cal grinned. "Right, if she has it," he said, putting *if* in air quotes, which made everyone in the room laugh.

Roman left the room with the phone to his ear, and Selina and Efren stood. "Since there's nothing we can do," Selina said. "We're going to the museum."

"The museum?" Cal asked in surprise.

"I heard that the Richard I. Bong Veterans Historical Center shouldn't be missed. It's in Superior near the harbor."

Cal smirked and dug into his pocket, tossing her some keys. "Have fun, you two lovebirds. Don't get caught doing something I wouldn't do."

"Hooah," Efren said as they left the room.

"Hooah?" Derek asked. "I thought that was what the Marines said."

"It means heard, understood and acknowledged," Cal said as he sat down. "H-U-A, but you say hooah. It's an army thing." He tapped the table to get them back on track. "Did you guys leave the room last night after you returned from the meeting with Detective Henry?"

"No," Alayah said. "We went back to the room and passed out until I got the all-call alert."

"Good, when we're done here, text Zac that information. What I want you and Derek to do is track Josh and his interactions in this hotel during the conference. Who did he talk to? How many calls did he make? What was his body language on those calls? That kind of thing. I also want you to dig into his company and see what you see. Derek should be able to help you with questions about apps, sales, mergers, or contacts, right?" he asked him, and Derek nodded.

"At least as much as my knowledge of the industry goes. I won't know the inner workings of his company, but we all deal with many of the same contacts, so I can help in that regard. What are you looking for exactly?"

"Any business dealings over the last year that may have angered someone enough to want Josh dead. A personal relationship that went bad over the last year or year and a half that was messy. A mistress who worked for a competing company or who had a secret. That kind of thing."

"Josh was a known player," Derek said with an eye roll. "That could take time."

"Which we don't have much of, so use your judgment. I'm hoping a pattern develops that will lead us in the right direction."

"I won't let you down, boss," Alayah said with a nod.

"We'll work on that until the camera footage comes in from the marina. Once it does, I'll break and search for any leads there. Do you want me to call you once I have the footage time-stamped with his movements?"

"Yes. I'll come up, and we'll talk in your room. The less we talk in areas under camera surveillance, the better. That's why we all crammed into my suite. I'm at the trust-no-one stage of this debacle."

"Can't blame you there," Derek said with a shake of his head. "This is madness that I never could've predicted a few days ago. We'll head back to the room now and get started."

With a nod from Cal, they left his room and headed to their own, both silent as they processed the information they'd just learned. Hugo Victor and Josh Hunt were murdered. That brought him back to the questions of why and by whom?

When they returned to their room, he set about ordering breakfast while Alayah logged on to her machines. He could tell she was aching to get to work, and so was he, something didn't sit right with Josh having gone to Superior for a hookup. Did Derek doubt for a second that he'd entertained someone while at the conference? No, that was totally on-brand for the guy, but Josh was always about the wining, dining and being seen with a beautiful woman on his arm and money in his hand. A houseboat in the middle of the night was a bit too sleazy for him. Especially when he had a posh hotel room. Unless the woman he was meeting was married, he supposed.

After he finished making each of them a cup of coffee, he carried hers to the desk. "Thanks," she said, glancing up at him with a smile when he set it down beside her.

"I ordered breakfast. It'll be here shortly."

"Good, I'm starving," she said, rubbing her belly. "I normally eat six times a day, which hasn't been possible here."

He rubbed her back and then leaned in to tease her lips in a gentle kiss. "Part of that is my fault, but I promise to make it up to you. Let me steal you away for a few days when this is over. I'll feed you good food, we can drink expensive wine and get to know each other better."

She didn't answer right away. Instead, she stared him down for several seconds before responding. "I'd love that more than anything, but it may not be a good idea, Derek."

"Because I deserve to be with someone who looks different than you? A woman who's 'normal?'" he asked, using air quotes. It was her sad nod that broke him.

"And a woman who can give you children. I've learned that men want to pass their name and DNA down for generations. The buck stops with me."

"This is the perfect example of why we should spend that time getting to know each other better," he said with a smile as he trailed a finger down her cheek. "For instance, I don't know who my father is. My mother does, but she's never told me, and honestly, since he's never had anything to do with me, it doesn't matter. My stepfather adopted me when I was four, and he was the only father I'd ever known until he passed away five years ago. Passing my DNA down means nothing to me. As for sharing my last name, any child I love, whether through surrogacy or adoption, would still bear my name. Family is family, no matter how it's made. Seems like you've already learned that being adopted as a child and now working for Secure Watch."

"Fair," she agreed with a small smile.

"And any guy who made you feel less than for something outside of your control is not a guy you'd want to share a life with anyway, in my opinion. You deserve so much more than that, sweetheart."

Then he gathered her into his arms and held her, praying that she understood he could be the one to offer her everything.

Chapter Twenty-One

Alayah clicked her way through the video feed as she searched for Josh in the hotel. According to Derek, neither he nor Hugo had seen him before he'd left for the cabin, but that didn't mean that Hugo hadn't seen him before he died. Derek swore that wasn't possible, but her line of work had taught her that anything was possible.

The remnants of their breakfast sat off to the side, but she continued to pick at the fruit as she worked. She'd learned to be a grazer, so you rarely saw her at work without food beside her. The team at Secure Watch had started grabbing her a snack and leaving it on her desk as they walked past. It reminded her of something Derek had said earlier about found family and how DNA mattered less than love. While he wasn't wrong, in her case, DNA did matter. It mattered because it made her life difficult, so why would she ask someone else to deal with those same frustrations and pain when they didn't have to?

Because sharing it with someone else can make the burden easier to bear.

She forced herself not to roll her eyes at the thought. It was nice in theory, but not so nice when the theory didn't work out, breaking her heart in the process. "What's that?" She paused the recording and pointed to the screen.

Derek leaned in and squinted. "I don't see anything." She backed it up again and slowed it down, pausing it again as she pointed to a shadow at the back of the stage. "It's probably one of the convention employees helping connect his mic."

They kept their eyes glued to the screen, hoping whoever was in the shadows would step out and be caught by the camera. Her finger darted out. "Look. Hugo is talking to the person, and his body language says he's not happy."

"Still doesn't mean it's Josh," Derek said. "Hugo is always a hot mess before speeches. You should have seen him before his TED Talk. I wasn't sure he would make it onstage, much less give the speech."

She punched a few buttons, and the screen went blank.

"What happened?" he asked, glancing at her in surprise.

"I'm changing to a different camera angle," she explained, waiting for the one to spool up to the time stamp she'd typed. "If we can see them from a different angle, we might be able to see what Hugo is saying."

When her screen loaded, it was too dark to see anything. "So much for that," she groaned, switching it back to the other camera. "We may not see who it is, but we know he interacted with someone before the speech."

They kept watching, surprised when the exchange heated even more, and the mystery person stepped forward.

Derek gasped. "That's Josh!"

Without thinking, she froze the frame. "You're sure?"

"Absolutely," he said. "He's all pretty-boy elite all the time. That fancy suit vest paired with a T-shirt and chinos is his signature look. I'd know him anywhere. You didn't see this the first time you played the video?"

"No," she said, grabbing her pen. "I never went this far. My job was to follow the water bottle, not Hugo. When I tracked you, I followed you through the hotel to backstage. Then, when you left Hugo, I followed you out of the convention center to the parking lot. Of note, I was working the comms when Hugo was having this discussion with Josh. We didn't hear any of this interaction."

She clicked the mouse again, and the video continued to play. Hugo and Josh gesticulated wildly for thirty more seconds before Josh disappeared and Hugo turned, his face masked with anger. After several calming breaths, he fiddled with something attached to his belt.

"There," Derek said. "He'd shut his mic off."

"That explains why we didn't hear them. Unfortunately, we can see their interaction but not hear it, which doesn't help us much."

"Other than knowing they fought about something. That's not new, though. They were oil and water, so it could have been about whether the sky was blue. They were basically children."

"Sounds like it," she said, shaking her head at the immaturity of some grown adults. She knew how common that was after working in the industry, but it still surprised her sometimes. Her email dinged, and she clicked on her inbox. "Looks like Mina got us that footage of Josh in Superior."

While she loaded it up, he leaned back in his chair. "Well, if nothing else, we know it wasn't Hugo who killed him."

"Fair point," she agreed, opening the file. "But someone did. However, I doubt we will get so lucky as to see their face on this video."

She pressed Play, and they watched as Josh parked his car and climbed out. He glanced around the area briefly, as though he wasn't sure what to do next.

"He's disheveled," Derek noticed. "The Josh I know

would never have gone out with his hair askew and wearing lounge pants."

"Someone rolled him out of bed," Alayah deduced, and Derek nodded. "The question is who and why?"

"And why did he jump when they said jump? Why didn't he take the time to get dressed?"

"He doesn't have a wife or kids, right?" Alayah asked to be sure. She assumed, but in this business, one must never make assumptions.

"Absolutely not. He thrived on his social image of being the man every woman wants," Derek said, watching the screen as Josh wandered the parking lot. He checked his phone before he walked to the edge of the lot and out of the frame.

"Great," Alayah muttered, calling up a map on an open webpage. "We need to know what's over there."

"Looks like not much of anything other than the public beach."

"There has to be a camera on the beach somewhere, right?" she asked, ready to dig in when he pointed to another image.

"Maybe, but look. There's a wooded area between the marina lot and the beach. I'd bet my last dollar the person he's meeting is in those trees."

"Like whoever it is knows where the cameras are?"

"Wouldn't you if you were planning to kill someone?"

"That's what gets me," she noted. "If this person planned to kill Josh, why pick this area to do it? It's off-season, so there aren't as many people around, but there's a highway on the other side of the slips. Anyone driving by could notice people walking around down there and remember them."

"You're saying they weren't planning to kill him?"

"Maybe they just wanted to talk, but things got out of hand?" she asked, and he shrugged.

"Anything is possible, I suppose."

She clicked back to the video. "We know it wasn't Hugo, so who else had enough disdain for Josh that a simple meeting ended in his death?"

"Half the people who knew and worked with him?" Derek suggested.

"So, you're saying he was well-liked," Alayah said, tongue in cheek. "Not super helpful."

"We don't have much, do we?" Derek asked, rubbing her tense shoulders to help her relax. "That gave us nothing."

"I wouldn't say that," she disagreed. "We know he didn't take time to prepare for the meeting, and he wasn't carrying anything except his phone. That makes me wonder where his phone ended up."

Unsure of her next move, she called Mina. "Secure Watch, Whiskey."

"Secure Watch, Alpha," she answered, shoulder-bumping Derek, who had unfortunately dropped his hands from her neck. She'd been enjoying his touch. She rarely got the pleasure of someone's touch who wasn't afraid to hurt her. Derek knew exactly what he could and couldn't do regarding her body. Sure, she'd made her condition clear, but he'd obviously paid attention and found other ways to offer her comfort because he wanted to, not because he had to. "You're on speaker."

"Did you watch the video?" Mina asked.

"Sure did," Alayah answered. "It was somewhat informative but wasn't super helpful."

"You found it informative? We got nothing."

"It could have been more helpful, but Derek pointed

out that Josh had jumped out of bed and driven to Superior without pause."

"We noticed the bedhead," Mina agreed with a chuckle. "We figured he got a surprise hookup phone call."

"You had to know the guy," Derek explained. "He never left the room if he wasn't spit-polished to a shine. He also didn't have his briefcase or computer with him. Was it in his car?"

"Don't know, but he'd have to have left it in there the night before. He wasn't carrying anything when he left the hotel at 0300 hours. We know he had his phone, but otherwise, it doesn't appear he took anything with him from the room."

"That's also a red flag," Derek said. "He had this leather attaché that I swear was glued to his hand. If this meeting was for business, he wouldn't have gone out without it."

"Which brings us back to a personal reason for being out there," Mina said.

"There weren't any other cameras available to pull from?" Alayah asked.

None that were usable. The other cameras are static, so if someone did push him into the water from that area, it wouldn't be caught on camera."

"Which is probably why whoever he was meeting picked that spot," Derek mused.

"Do we know where he was found in the harbor? Was he near that wooded area or somewhere else?" Alayah asked.

"He was found floating near a small bridge just down from the beach. It wouldn't be impossible for him to float that far in the amount of time he was in the water. I'm currently trying to get footage from the camera at the beach to see if there's a time stamp of him floating past."

"To say we're dead in the water until then is a bit on

the nose?" Alayah asked, smiling when Derek covered his mouth with his hand to maintain his composure. "Or maybe we should consider this a dead end?"

"Alayah," Mina said, trying to bite back laughter. "You're killing me here."

They all broke into a fit of giggles brought on by too little sleep and raw nerves.

"I'm sorry, that was inappropriate. A man is dead, and that's nothing to make fun of. I'm just frustrated by the lack of evidence. Our business is to find proof of these crimes. What are we missing?"

"Wait. Our business is to find proof of these crimes," Derek repeated. "Almost as though whoever is behind this knows how not to leave any digital evidence behind."

"Because he works in the industry?" Mina asked.

"It's possible!" Alayah exclaimed. "This town is crawling with tech bros right now."

It was Mina's turn to laugh. "Tech bros. I know how much you love them." Alayah didn't interject to say there was one whom she was growing rather fond of. "Derek, do you know any other businesses that may have had issues with Josh?"

Alayah wasn't sure if Mina heard Derek's scoff, but she sure did.

"Open up Google, type in 'tech companies,' and pick one. You'll find someone who had an issue with Josh. Hugo included. Their history is well known in the industry as we discussed."

"A very likable kind of guy, apparently. Always the worst kind in life and death. Death because it's hard to narrow down the field of potential killers when everyone was a hater."

"That sums it up well," Derek agreed. "I wouldn't dig

too deep into Hugo and Josh's feud, other than to look for any commonalities between them regarding employees or shared close business consultants. If it would help, I could come up with the top five companies with a bigger bone to pick with him than most."

"As long as we don't have to track their whereabouts down," Alayah clarified. "Cal wants us to make notes of everyone Josh talked to at the conference, and we're just getting started with that. That doesn't include looking into his business dealings to see if there are any red flags there."

"Let me start with that aspect of the dig," Mina said. "If I start looking into his business dealings, that will naturally reveal people he had issues with and may have angered. I'll assign several people to work on it, and once we have the names, I'll forward them to you. With that information in hand, Derek can tell us the strongest trails to follow. It will also help you rule in or out interactions that you may witness with people on the footage from the conference."

"That would be a huge help," Alayah confirmed. "The faster we can get the information to Cal, the better. Let's face it, it can't be a coincidence that the opening and closing speakers of this conference were killed. There's a connection somewhere. We need to find it. Let's use our Messenger app to exchange information in real time."

"You got it. Whiskey, out."

Alayah disconnected the call and turned to Derek. "We make a great team."

"We sure do," he said with a genuine smile. "Now, while you spool up the camera feed, I'll make us more coffee. The faster we figure out who killed Hugo and Josh, the faster I can take you out on a real date."

"I don't remember you asking to take me out on a real

date," she answered, batting her lashes coyly. He had, but this time, she had a different answer for him.

He turned back and knelt, taking her hand in his. "Alayah Heath, would you do me the pleasure of going out on a real date where we eat good food, drink great wine and talk about anything other than computers or tech bros?"

Her laughter filled the room, but she melted into a pile of goo on the inside. "I would love to."

Chapter Twenty-Two

Derek knocked on Cal's door, offering Alayah a smile as they waited. It was late, but they'd done what he'd asked and tracked Josh through the entire conference until he'd left for the final time last night.

The door opened and Cal motioned them in. "I was starting to worry you'd fallen asleep."

"Sorry, boss," Alayah said, and Derek noticed her grimace. It hadn't been her fault, and he jumped to defend her.

"It's been a lot of back-and-forth with Secure Watch to find the information and then to verify it."

Cal held up his hand. "I apologize for saying that. I'm frustrated with the lack of movement on the case. Not from lack of trying but from lack of evidence. I know everyone is doing their best to find something that will bring this all together and make it make sense."

"For all our work, we don't have much," Alayah agreed, opening her laptop and setting it on the bed, which was the perfect height for her to use while standing. She'd mentioned to him on the way over how tired she was of sitting, and he vowed to grab some food and let her walk around the hotel a bit once they finished here. Then, he'd take her back to the room for a shower and bed. He just hoped she'd be in his bed again tonight because he loved nothing more than holding her as he dropped off to sleep. He found a sense of safety being with her that he'd never experienced with any other woman. That spoke to his heart in more ways than one.

"You're not helping my mood much," Cal said with a chuckle.

"Trust me, we both agree," Derek said. "However, with Mina's help, it was easy to alibi all the tech bros that Josh encountered at the convention. That part hadn't been too hard since he hadn't done his presentation yet and the convention had only been up and running for one full day. If there were interactions at his hotel or in the community, we wouldn't know because we don't have access to his schedule or the hotel feeds from his hotel."

"That's fair. Nothing stood out to you as a negative confrontation?" Cal asked.

"Only one," Alayah said, clicking the mouse and letting the footage play of Hugo and Josh backstage.

"That was right before Hugo died?"

"Yes. I didn't know it was there since I stopped watching that part of the feed to track Derek once he left Hugo backstage," Alayah explained. "But if you look closely, Hugo turns his mic off before arguing with Josh and then back on after the exchange. We never would've heard their interaction from the control booth."

"Too bad. It would be nice to know what they said."

Derek lowered himself to the bed next to her computer. "It was probably the same old song and dance where Josh wanted to buy the new cyber app, but Hugo wouldn't sell. I could repeat it verbatim, but I'll spare you the details. Suffice it to say Hugo was tired of the constant emails and contact from Virtual Scorpion Productions about it. He swore Josh had everyone on his staff email us every week."

"Reeks of desperation to me," Alayah said, shaking her head.

"Wait, what?" Derek asked and Alayah glanced at him.

"I said it reeks of desperation. Why did he need Black Marlin's app so badly if he could create his own?"

"She's right," Cal said, crossing his arms over his chest. "Did we ever get his financials?"

"We got some, but Mina is still working on getting everything. That's easier said than done with a company that knows how to protect its servers. Nothing she's found so far has set off any alarms. The company had plenty of money, and there were no mergers or any evidence of an attempted coup."

"For all intents and purposes, Virtual Scorpion was the next Black Marlin," Derek confirmed. "I always assumed that the reason Josh wanted the app was to merge the two companies and make it a powerhouse in the industry."

"Would Hugo have gone for that?" Cal asked.

"Absolutely not. He always called Josh a gnat on the bottom of his shoe. Just to be extra annoying, he pronounced the *g* every time." He smiled at the memory, and the part of him who would miss his boss in his day-to-day life reared its head again. He was grateful when Alayah reached over and took his hand in hers, squeezing his fingers. It helped him focus again.

"Then we're missing something," Cal said. "There had to be a reason Josh was so desperate to get the app. From the interaction I just saw between them, that is the word to describe it."

"Running out in the middle of the night in your pajamas to a deserted parking lot also suggests that," Alayah said. "Did you get any new details about Josh's death since our last check-in?"

"All we know is that his manner of death was blunt force trauma to the head. The autopsy revealed he was already dead when he hit the water, as there was none in his lungs."

"Which means there won't be a murder weapon to find," Derek said with a groan.

"Cops thought it was probably a rock, which is likely now at the bottom of Lake Superior."

"Did the cops offer up that information willingly?" Derek asked, and Cal shook his head with a grin.

"Selina was a cop back in the day, and she's good at talking the talk and walking the walk. She's extremely skilled at drawing information from the cops by letting them think she is one."

"That's why they wanted to go to Superior this morning!" Derek exclaimed, smacking his hand to his forehead. "Well, at least it wasn't a wasted trip."

"I would say it's a perfect crime, but there's no such thing," Alayah said, still typing away on the computer. "We all know that, but our hands are tied a little tighter because Virtual Scorpion didn't hire us. Had they done that, we could access everything, but not when we're trying to siphon information from other sources that are built to protect that information."

"This might be one we have to let the cops solve, but I want my people cleared so we can leave," Cal groused. "This has been an unmitigated disaster in multiple ways."

Derek could understand why Cal felt that way. It was true for him as well in all but one way. One small but very significant way, and her name was Alayah.

Fingers tapping on the mouse pad, Alayah tipped her head side to side as though stretching her neck, but he'd seen her do this multiple times before and knew she was thinking. "We're missing something. Do we have Hugo's autopsy report yet?"

Cal shook his head. "No, they had to run tox screens on him, so it takes longer. We know he died from antifreeze ingestion, but the cops want to know if there was anything else in his system."

"I need to talk to Mina," Alayah said, drumming her fingers on the bed.

Cal grabbed his phone and called Mina, going through their usual greeting before putting it on speakerphone. "What's up?"

"We're missing something with Josh's financials. Did we check his personal finances or just Virtual Scorpion's?" Alayah asked.

"They're tied together," Mina answered. "At least, from what we could find."

"Would you check again?"

"What are you looking for?"

Derek wasn't sure if she asked because she was skeptical or to gauge the situation.

"A reason why he'd need this app that Hugo was bringing to market. We know the business didn't need capital, but there had to be a reason he wanted an app that, according to Derek, was far better than one he could develop himself."

"You're thinking blackmail?" Mina asked.

"That or a secret baby momma who was bleeding him dry to stay quiet about having his kid. I don't know, but I know we're missing something."

"Okay, I trust you, Alayah. Give me some time. Whiskey, out."

Alayah closed her laptop. "I wish there was more we could do, Cal. I feel as helpless as you do right now. Unfortunately, my options are limited with the equipment I have on the premises, so we have to depend on Secure Watch to help."

Cal patted her back gently. "They will. If there's something to find, they'll find it. In the meantime, why don't you get some rest—"

Whatever else he was going to say was interrupted by a knock on the door. Cal walked to it and checked the peephole before pulling it open. Derek recognized both men standing at the door. Ryland Frye, the defense attorney Cal had sent a few nights ago, stood beside Anthony Duffy, the attorney for Black Marlin Technologies. He stood slowly as the men walked into the room.

"Anthony? What are you doing here?"

"Mr. Duffy reached out to me to help him facilitate this meeting," Ryland explained. "He has some interesting things to say that may change the picture here."

"First of all, I want to say how sorry I am to hear about Hugo's death. I know you two were close."

"As were you," Derek said with a nod. "I'm sure you were equally pained to lose a good friend."

"He was a good friend, but as I was his attorney, I was privy to certain attorney-client privileges the rest of the board wasn't. When I was notified of his death, I returned to Minneapolis immediately from my vacation to deal with the situation."

"I still don't understand why you're here," Derek said. "My involvement with Black Marlin Technologies ended with Hugo's death. I assured Curtis I would turn in my badge upon my return. He already stripped me of my login rights, so I can't access any company records."

"I heard," he said with an eye roll. "I spoke with the board and informed them that they must continue to run things as usual while I sorted out Hugo's will. I assured them once that was done, we would get together to discuss our next steps. However, I already knew what Hugo's will stated."

"I'm confused," Derek said, glancing between the lawyers. "If you already knew what the will said, why didn't you tell the board? Again, my employment with Black Marlin ended with Hugo's death."

"Your employment, yes," Anthony agreed. "However, you are Hugo's sole beneficiary. You now own Black Marlin Technologies."

"HEY, YOU'RE OKAY," Alayah said, taking Derek's hands after he sat. "Take a deep breath with me." She inhaled and waited for him to do the same before she blew it back out again. After they had spoken with Hugo's attorney, Derek asked to return to their room. She couldn't blame him, considering the bombshell that Anthony had dropped.

"Why didn't Hugo tell me he was leaving the company to me?" he asked again, even though Anthony had answered the question several times.

"Plausible deniability," she said, hoping that would make it easier for him to grasp than how the lawyer had explained it. "If you didn't know that's what he was going to do, you couldn't tell anyone."

"Curtis is going to be livid. I wouldn't doubt if he takes this to court."

"Isn't he just an employee?" she asked in surprise. "You made it sound like Hugo owned the business."

"Curtis is a board member and is employed as the chief financial officer, so while he doesn't have any control over the company, he controls the coffers." He stood to pace around the room. "I don't know if I even want the company.

I'm tired of living in the city, not to mention I don't want to become consumed by work like Hugo was."

"He left you the company to do with as you wish. You could sell it," she suggested. "Either way, he's set you up for life financially, which is what he wanted, according to the lawyer."

Derek ran his hands down his face and sighed. "That's true, and I'm grateful. I'm extremely grateful, but I'm not looking forward to dealing with the board. After that last phone call with Curtis, it won't go well. A confrontation with him could get ugly."

"It could, so I think it's smart that you take Anthony's suggestion and address the board together. You don't have to do any of this alone. I may not understand how you're feeling right now, but I do know that, despite the issues that come with inheriting a company like Black Marlin Technologies, it's important to remember that Hugo loved you above anyone else. He had to, to trust you with the one thing he spent his entire life building. There's something to be said for celebrating that kind of love, right?"

He dropped his hand from his hair as a breath left his chest. "I hadn't thought of it that way, but it's true. We should celebrate that aspect of it a little bit. Hugo would want that."

"He would, and since we're on hold while we wait for Mina to find us another avenue to investigate, why don't we grab a shower and have dinner? Room service? Or do you want to go out?"

"Go out to eat or stay in and eat dinner in bed with you? Not even a hard call. Dinner in bed with you," he said, pecking her lips.

"I didn't say anything about dinner in bed," she teased, enjoying his playfulness.

"You didn't have to," he assured her as he stood and kissed her hand. "Your eyes told me what they want. I hope my eyes tell you that I want you."

"If your eyes don't, your lips do," she promised as he leaned down for another kiss. "Go grab a shower while I order dinner."

"Thank you," he whispered, his lips near hers again.

"I can handle ordering dinner, Derek."

"Not for dinner, but for being you. For keeping me calm when my world spun off into orbit and I couldn't orient myself again. For believing in me when people I've known for years don't anymore."

She put her finger to his lips until he quieted. "The people who matter still believe in you, Derek Benjamin. You're a good person, and that is evidenced by Hugo's gift today. If I know you, and I think I know you somewhat well by now, you'll use that gift for good. I can't wait to watch it all unfold."

"Are you sticking around, Alayah Heath?" he asked, stroking her cheek tenderly.

"At least until you get sick of me and send me packing." As scary as that was to admit, it was time she did. Maybe she hadn't known him for long, but the way she felt about him didn't need time. It was there the moment they met.

"That will never happen," he promised.

Never say never, was all she could think.

Chapter Twenty-Three

Alayah held up her glass. "To Hugo."

"To Hugo," Derek whispered, clinking his glass to hers. "May he rest in peace."

They swallowed the wine and set their glasses aside. The food had been delicious, and now, she was full, happy and enjoying being snuggled up in bed with Derek without any demands on her time.

"Do you get tired of eating kids' food?" he asked, stroking her arm.

"Are you saying corn dogs and chicken strips aren't for the refined palate?"

His laughter tickled her ears, and she smiled. If she could keep him laughing, then maybe the shock of inheriting a multibillion-dollar business would feel less overwhelming. Derek had an appointment tomorrow morning with Anthony to go over everything with him and put a formal proposal together for the board. Anthony asked Derek to think about how he wanted to frame things, and she was hoping food and wine would relax him so he could look at it objectively. "I just wondered if I could cook for you and make things you've wanted to try but don't want to have ten servings left over."

"You couldn't know this, but at Secure Inc., we have a

resident chef. She prepares three meals a day and keeps the extremely hungry security personnel well-fed. Mostly, she cooks buffet-style, so I can take as little as I want. However, when she makes steaks or burgers on the grill, she always makes one for me that's smaller. When I'm out on jobs, I stick to the kids' menus if I don't have a way to keep the food for a few days. It's never for an extended period, so I don't mind."

"I didn't know that about Secure Inc., though I shouldn't be surprised. Cal seems to have everything in hand when it comes to keeping that place running smoothly."

"He hasn't always," she admitted. "But as the company grew, he had no choice but to figure out ways to grow with it. Many of the Secure Watch employees work remotely, but I'm fortunate to have a room at Secure Inc. It's a great place for someone like me to work."

"Someone like you? Someone who is amazingly brilliant and scary good at her job, not to mention a beautiful person inside and out?"

Her smile was wide when she turned to him. "Are you trying to butter me up, Mr. Benjamin?"

"Nope," he said, tracing her lips with his finger. "Just speaking the truth. From what I've seen over the last few days, you consistently underestimate your skills and yourself. I want to be the one who points out how truly remarkable you are so that one day, you'll believe it too."

"'Remarkable' is what they put on my chart at the hospital. A remarkably complicated case."

"A remarkably resilient woman who deserves to be happy and enjoy life," he corrected, stealing a kiss. His tasted like sweet wine and she moaned as he dipped his tongue in to taste hers. Her hand was tangled in his shirt, and she gasped for air when he finally released her lips. "Say you believe that, or I'll keep kissing you until you do."

"I absolutely do not and will never believe that," she whispered with a sly smile.

"I warned you," he teased before his lips attacked hers again. She wrapped her hand behind his head to hold his neck while his hand wandered to stroke up and down her rib cage. Each time he got dangerously close to her breasts, she inhaled a sharp breath, both wanting and not wanting him to touch her there. She yearned for his touch but knew he'd be disappointed by what he found, which wasn't much of anything. "Stop thinking," he scolded, his lips still on hers. "Whatever it is, it can wait."

"Not really," she replied. Since his lips were on hers, she didn't have to look into his eyes, which gave her the courage to say what had to be said. "I was thinking about how disappointed you'll be if you move your hand three inches to the left."

"Like this?" he asked, sliding his hand from her rib cage to her chest.

The sensation was foreign after so long without a man's touch, and she had to steady her breathing before she answered.

"Not much to see, right?" she asked, but rather than answer, he simply put his lips back on hers and kissed her breathless while his hand lay flat against her chest. His warmth soaked into her and somehow healed parts of her she hadn't realized were broken. If they parted ways and she never saw him again, she would be thankful to him for the rest of her life for that.

"A woman's body is always something to see," he said, kissing his way across her chin and down her neck.

"But you've never seen a body like mine," she promised.

"I won't deny that," he said, running his tongue along her collarbone until she shuddered. "Doesn't mean I don't want to. I know you think you're not worthy of being worshipped like any other woman, but you're wrong. You deserve to be worshipped and ravished."

"And you're the man for the job?" she asked, to which he gave her a naughty grin.

"I sure as hell hope so."

"Prove it," she said, lifting her arms over her head. "Take my shirt off and prove it."

Without a word, he grasped the hem of her shirt and then tenderly pulled it over her head to reveal her chest. She waited for him to say something, anything, but he just stared at her bare skin until goose bumps lifted across her torso.

"Derek, you don't—"

He put his finger to her lips and lowered his head, where he kissed every inch of her skin, including the long scar that ran between her breasts. When he was finished, he lavished her nipples with his tongue to warm them until she was writhing under his hands. Before she realized it, he had worked her pants down past her hips, leaving her naked and open to his searching gaze.

"So damn beautiful," he said, kissing his way down her belly.

"Why am I the only one without clothes on?" she squeaked as he ran his finger through the soft hair at her apex.

"I've been too busy taking off yours," he answered, reluctantly pulling away to strip himself of his clothes. The sight before her was a solid reminder of how much bigger he was.

"So damn handsome," she said, reaching up to touch his face when he bent for a kiss.

"Bruises and all?"

"Bruises and all," she agreed, letting her hand wander to touch and feel his velvety skin under hers. Leveraging herself upward, she sat to feather kisses across his chest, taking time to trail her tongue along his sensitive spots the way he had hers.

When she reached his navel, she dipped her tongue in for a moment before kissing lower until she could place one on his tip, drawing an exclaimed gasp from his lips. Rather than back off, she continued kissing, licking and suckling as his moans of pleasure filled the room. His body shook with the effort it took to hold back and let her explore him the way he had her.

When he groaned long and low, she glanced up, worried by his expression. "It just hit me that I don't have any condoms," he whispered.

"I can't get pregnant, and I'm clean," she answered before running her tongue down his shaft.

"I'm clean, too, but I want you to understand that I do respect you. We can wait until I have condoms if that makes you more comfortable."

"I trust you, Derek. Maybe that's nuts after only knowing you a few days, but you've given me every reason to trust you."

"That's the first time someone didn't say you've given me no reason not to trust you."

"When you're my size, actions speak much louder than words. There is a difference between showing someone they can trust you and telling someone they can trust you."

His lips were on hers as he leaned over, ramping up their desire until she thought she'd combust. "Derek," she moaned. "Please."

"I won't hurt you?" he asked, lifting his lips to hold her

gaze. Maybe he was searching for honesty, so she'd give it to him.

"Physically? No. Emotionally?"

Before she could finish, his lips were on hers again as his hand moved between her legs to prepare her for their joining. "Also no," he murmured.

"You can't know that. We haven't known each other that long."

Rather than respond immediately, he continued to stroke her until she lifted her hips, showing him how ready she was to be with him.

"To be clear, I don't sleep with women I've only known a few days. At least, I haven't until tonight. I have strong feelings for you—stronger than I've had for any other woman in my life—and in a completely different way. Maybe that doesn't make sense to you, but it does to me. That's what tells me this is right."

"When you know you know?" she whispered, but rather than answer, he rolled to the side and gently lifted her to straddle him. As they locked gazes, she saw the answer to that question. He knew, and now he would give her time to accept him with her body and her heart.

ALAYAH WOKE SLOWLY, her body warm and tingly as she cuddled into Derek's side. He'd been so incredibly tender during their lovemaking that she'd wanted to cry. It wasn't just his touch but the way he made love to her with his eyes. When he told her how beautiful she was and how lucky he was to be part of her life, she realized that she'd never made love to any other man. They'd shared their bodies, but not their minds or their hearts. That wasn't the case with Derek. They'd opened themselves up and shared everything. For her, that included the parts of herself she never let anyone see. He saw it all, kissed it all, and changed her unequivocally for life.

Her gaze strayed to the clock, and she was surprised to see it was after eleven. As much as she wanted to stay snuggled up next to him, she needed to check in with Mina. It had been hours since their request for Secure Watch to dive into Josh's business. They might not have anything yet, but it was her job to be sure. The moment they had a path to follow, she had to work quickly if they wanted to end this and return to their normal lives. Not that hers would mean much without Derek, but he deserved a chance to do big things.

Slowly, Alayah scooted away from him, his hard body now soft and relaxed in sleep. She hoped he was getting the rest he needed to plot a new course for his life, however unexpected that might now be. It would be a life she would never be part of. As much as she had enjoyed their time together, city life wasn't for her, and neither was working with tech moguls. She'd been there, done that, and couldn't do it again. Did the idea of losing what they could be together make her sad? Terribly so, considering she had fallen for him hook, line and sinker. Regardless, Alayah would never ask him to give up an opportunity like Black Marlin Technologies. Hugo wanted him to have his company, and he had worked hard for it, even if he hadn't come to that realization yet. She would never ask him to compromise or give up his dream if that was what he wanted. Sure, Minneapolis was only six hours from Secure Inc., but long-distance relationships rarely work. Determined, she put all the "what-ifs" from her mind so she could find a killer who was determined to stay hidden. If she couldn't share her life with Derek, at least she could be the hero he needed right now.

Once she had shimmied off the bed, she scooped her

phone off the nightstand and closed the bedroom door behind her. After a quick shower, she threw on a pair of warm pajamas and checked her phone. Mina had left a message that she should check her email ASAP.

Excited, she fired up her machine and clicked open the email, hoping they'd found something on Josh. It only took her a few seconds of scanning the files to let out a soft whistle. They'd hit the motherload. Josh was up to his ears in debt and sinking fast. Now she just had to figure out why.

Chapter Twenty-Four

Alayah leaned back in her chair to ponder the information she'd read from Mina's sources. Josh's business was more than profitable, so why was he so deep in debt? Where was the money going? He had a nice house and car, but otherwise owned nothing extravagant that would indicate a spending problem. Maybe he was a gambler? There was a note at the bottom from Mina stating that he'd taken out a predatory loan by every definition. When it came due in a few months, it would put him under. Especially if Hugo's app was released first and better appealed to consumers. Since Hugo planned to release the app free, that put another big wrinkle in Josh's plan. Logically, the first order of business was to contemplate if the debt Josh carried had gotten him killed. According to Derek, Hugo hadn't told anyone that he planned to release the app for free. At least not anyone outside of the company, but she couldn't help but wonder if he had told Josh and that was why they were fighting backstage.

It was time to dig in and figure out what part of Josh's life was the contributing factor to his death. Gambling debts would make sense. If he owed money to the wrong people, he would probably do everything in his power to pay them off, even if it meant taking out a loan with less than favorable terms.

Head in her work, she began tracing his financials and his whereabouts. Were the conferences he attended held at big casinos? Were there rumors that he'd been invited to any behind-closed-doors, high-stakes poker games? Every avenue she went down led her to a dead end in that respect. If Josh had been gambling, it wasn't blatant. Sports betting was a possibility, but looking at his life, he didn't have any interest in sports, so the knowledge to make educated bets probably wasn't there. Not that he couldn't be paying someone to do it for him, but his financials didn't reflect that either. They had to be missing something.

Blackmail.

The one word floated through Alayah's head in such a way that her fingers froze on the keyboard. Blackmail would explain why he was so far in debt with nothing to show for it. The money was coming from somewhere, but since they couldn't see all his business accounts, she couldn't be sure if he was siphoning off the business funds or using his own. She also couldn't see if he was taking large sums at once or wiring funds in smaller amounts to someone.

She grabbed her phone, knowing Mina would still be awake. She wanted to run it past someone else before she wasted too much time. She glanced at the bedroom door and sighed. Waking Derek by talking on the phone didn't appeal, so she set the phone down again. They had two dead tech giants on their hands for no apparent reason. What was the reason?

Almost as though whoever is behind this knows how not to leave any digital evidence behind.

Derek's comment from earlier in the day slammed into her. Someone was scrubbing the digital evidence. It was there, but it was hidden just like when they'd made it look like Derek was responsible for Hugo's death. Someone had access to the hotel servers, both theirs and the one Josh was at. Not surprising considering the virtual lack of security on these systems, but regardless, planting code to cover your movements was next-level diabolical and extremely purposeful. Whoever was behind it was known in the industry and was attempting to hide behind a digital cloak.

Her phone rang, and she grabbed it instantly. "Secure Watch, Alpha," she whispered.

"Secure Watch, Whiskey. Why are you whispering?" Mina asked as Alayah hopped down and walked to the balcony to step out into the cool night air.

"Derek is asleep and I don't want to wake him. He needs the rest as he tries to process what happened today."

"I heard Hugo left him the company. That had to be… jarring."

"To say the least," Alayah agreed. "He's had a lot thrown at him in the last few days."

"Derek is lucky to have found a friend in you at the time he needed you most, Alayah."

Her entire system froze for a moment as her brain floundered for words. It felt like a trap to her, and considering what happened just a few hours ago, she could never let Mina think it was anything more than friendship. At least not until this was over and she was back in the safety of Secure Inc.'s borders.

"I'm glad we've been able to help clear his name. He and Hugo were close, and he doesn't deserve to be treated like a criminal while trying to mourn his death."

Alayah held her breath. Would that answer pass muster?

Mina cleared her throat. "About that. What I uncovered puts him back under suspicion."

"How? We cleared him, Mina."

"You know we've been waiting to get Hugo's autopsy report, but had to wait for the toxicology screenings to return."

"Yes, but what does that have to do with Derek?"

"Well, I just got Hugo's autopsy report. Don't ask me how. It may not have been entirely legal." Alayah chuckled but waited for her to continue. "Hugo died of a massive heart attack from ingesting a large bolus of antifreeze."

"We already knew that."

"We did, but what we didn't know was that the coroner notes evidence that Hugo had been being poisoned slowly with microdoses of ethylene glycol for at least a month. It was only a matter of time before Hugo died, but for whatever reason, someone decided dying on stage would be a show no one wanted to miss."

"It wasn't Derek," she said immediately and without thought.

"You can't know that, Alayah."

"I can," she said, vibrating with anger that, once again, the man she had fallen for was facing unfounded accusations. "He's shown me who he is, and a cold-blooded killer is not who he is."

"Unfortunately, all arrows point to him. He was the one who had access to Hugo at all times. That came straight from him. They were joined at the hip. I know you don't want to hear that, but it's true."

"He's not the only one, though. Hugo worked in an office where plenty of people would have the opportunity to slip something in his coffee or food. If anything, it helps Derek's case."

"Okay, I trust your gut on this one," Mina said, and Alayah could hear the sincerity in her words. She wasn't placating her. "If you want my help, I'll need the names of the top people he thinks have the chops to do something like this, so we can dig into their background."

"Give me ten to wake him up and explain, and I'll get back to you. Alpha, out."

She hung up the phone and walked back into the room to puzzle out another twist in the game.

DEREK HAD WOKEN with a start when he heard a phone ring. Immediately, he realized he was alone, so he threw on his clothes and opened the bedroom door. The light was on by the desk, but Alayah was nowhere to be seen. Panic spiked through him. Where was she? Did their lovemaking scare her so much that she took off? He suspected she would second-guess herself, but not to the point she'd leave in the middle of the night. Then it filtered through his still half-asleep brain that her computer was on the desk and open. She'd obviously been using it. Then he spotted her on the balcony, phone to her ear. Her phone was what had woken him. With a relieved sigh, he leaned against the wall to wait for her so he could coax her back to bed. The rest of her work could wait until morning. After making love to her twice, he should be sated, but he'd quickly realized that might never be something he felt when it came to Alayah Heath. Every time he touched her, he wanted more. The idea of the "whole package" was a concept people floated around, but Derek had never experienced it until last night. Alayah was the whole package. Small in size but mighty in every other aspect of life.

"Derek," she said, and he realized he'd been daydreaming. "Did I wake you?"

He ran his hand down his face and shook his head. "No, I woke up and you were nowhere to be found. Come back to bed. Work can wait until tomorrow." The look that crossed her face had him pausing halfway to her. "What?"

She motioned for him to join her on the couch, so he sat, leaning in for a kiss. It was simply too hard to resist those lips when he knew what they could do.

"That was Mina on the phone."

"I figured," he agreed. "She was looking at Josh's financials, right?"

"Yes, and she sent me that stuff. He was in serious debt that would have destroyed his business if he didn't do something fast."

Derek tipped his head. "Why was he in debt? Virtual Scorpion Productions wasn't the size of Black Marlin Technologies, but he did very well for himself."

"I was in the middle of trying to find out when Mina called," she explained. "She got her hands on Hugo's preliminary autopsy report."

"I'm sure there was nothing surprising, right? He died of antifreeze poisoning."

"He died of a massive heart attack due to a large bolus of it, according to the coroner. However, there was evidence in his system that he'd been microdosed with antifreeze for weeks before his death."

The blood whooshed through his ears as he tried to make sense of what she'd just said. "I don't understand."

"According to the coroner, someone had been giving him small doses of antifreeze every day. Probably in his coffee or vitamin water."

"And Mina thinks it was me."

"I assured her it wasn't," Alayah said, squeezing his hand to keep him grounded.

He fumbled for his phone, pulling it from his pocket and opening an internet tab. "What are the symptoms of antifreeze poisoning? Hugo had been sick for at least a month with concerning symptoms."

"You mentioned that," she said, snapping her fingers. "You said he was forgetful and generally not healthy."

"Look," he said, pointing to the phone. "Forgetfulness, stomach pain and vomiting, heart palpitations, red skin and confusion. He had all these symptoms, and they were getting worse."

"As you'd expect to happen the longer he was exposed to the poison," she agreed. "You may have had the opportunity, but so did a lot of other people. Mina would like you to make a list of people who had means and opportunity."

"Curtis."

"Curtis?" she repeated and he nodded. "You think Curtis is behind this?"

"He's been angry at Hugo for refusing to take the company public." But was he angry enough to try to poison his boss? That was a stretch even for him, which Alayah echoed when she spoke.

"What good would it do to kill Hugo, though? We already know that none of them knew who he'd leave the business to."

"The only thing we know is that Hugo didn't tell anyone he was leaving it to me. We don't know—"

"That he didn't lie about who he was leaving the business to."

He gave her a nod, and she popped up off the sofa and hurried to the computer, jumping up into her seat and shaking the mouse to wake the screen.

"What are you doing?" he asked, walking over to stand beside her. He always wanted to stand beside her, even once this was resolved. All he had to do was figure out how.

"Before Mina called, I was tracing Josh's financials to

see if he had gambling debts or if he was being blackmailed."

"What does that have to do with Curtis?"

"Well, if your business was in trouble, what would make you jump out of bed at three a.m. and drive somewhere in your pajamas without taking the time to get dressed?"

"Money," he answered without thinking.

"What if he wasn't being blackmailed, but he was doing the blackmailing? Theoretically, it would solve his money problem."

"You think that Josh somehow knew that Curtis killed Hugo and wanted a payoff to stay quiet?"

"Would you put it past either of them?"

"Nope," he answered with a shake of his head. "That would be well within both of their personalities. Unfortunately, we can't prove it."

"Curtis is a board member, but also the CFO of Black Marlin Technologies, right?" she asked, and he nodded. "If we dig into Black Marlin's financials and see money being funneled to places it shouldn't be, that would prove it."

"It would prove that money was going somewhere it shouldn't, but not where or to whom. The only way to prove it's Curtis is to find him in Duluth before Hugo's murder, when he was supposed to be in California. I don't want to dig around in Black Marlin's files without consulting Anthony. It could screw something up with the transfer of the business. I can't risk it."

"You can't risk losing the business, but you'd risk letting your boss's killer go free?" Alayah asked, her jaw dropping open in shock and disappointment.

Rather than jump on her distrust, he took a moment to think about what he'd said. He heard what she'd heard once he ran it back through his head. With a caress to her cheek and then a finger under her chin to close her lips, he answered. "What I meant is, I can't risk *you* getting caught up in it. I know Secure Watch has ways to go undetected, but not from your computer or this hotel, whether using a VPN or not. Can Mina do it while we find Cal and bring him up to speed?"

"Easily. By the time anyone realizes someone has accessed the system, she'll already be out with the information in hand. Hang on," she said, opening her Messenger app and typing.

He watched her work and wondered how he got so damn lucky to have found her at the worst time of his life. The bigger question was how he would keep her when the case ended.

Chapter Twenty-Five

They'd been looking for Cal for fifteen minutes. Where could he be at this time of night? They'd tried his room, the gym, and the conference room.

"Maybe he went out for a walk?" Derek suggested as they stood in the hallway. "It's a beautiful night."

"It's also almost one a.m.," she answered. "Maybe he was sleeping and didn't hear us knock. Let me text him. We'll bang on his door again if he doesn't respond."

She sent the text and checked her messages while they waited. Mina had agreed to hack into Black Marlin's server to look for the information they needed before morning. If Derek was right, and Curtis was behind the murder of both Hugo and Josh, they'd need proof before they could ever convince the police. Hell, even with the information, it would be a tough sell to convince the cops to look at him. Then again, if Mina could find video footage of Curtis not getting on the plane to California, that might break the case wide open. At the very least, it would give Alayah a reason to search for Curtis in Duluth over the last three days.

Had it only been three days since his world had fallen apart and yet, oddly enough, been brought back together by a woman with the courage of a lion and a heart of gold? This week had taught him that time was something everyone thought they had more of. If that wasn't something to draw him up short, he didn't know what would. It was a reminder that he couldn't let Black Marlin Technologies take over his life the way it had Hugo's. He didn't want that kind of life. He wanted more. He wanted Alayah.

Alayah's phone rang and she held her finger up to him as she answered. While she talked to whoever was on the line, he wandered through the empty door of the convention hall to stare at the stage where his boss, the man who saw him as a son, had taken his last breath. It was another example of time changing the way we looked at things. The last time he'd been in this hall, he was ready to be done with Hugo and Black Marlin. The long hours and Hugo's heavy dependence had weighed heavily on him, but suddenly, he'd accept it all onto his shoulders again if it meant Hugo was still part of this world. That was the grief talking, but he still felt guilty for cutting and running on his boss. Did he deserve time off? Yes, but that didn't soothe the burn.

Nearly to the stage, he was surprised when the door above him closed with a snap. He whirled, expecting to see Alayah, but the person standing at the top of the stairs was not her.

"Pondering how our illustrious boss felt in the last few moments of his life? I hope it was the way he made us feel every day. Small and insignificant."

"What are you doing here?" Derek asked in shock as he stared down the very last person he'd expect to see in Duluth at nearly 1:00 a.m.

"Cleaning up messes and taking out the trash. I can't decide if you're the former or the latter or both. Either way, you gotta go."

It wasn't until she pulled out the gun that Derek's blood ran cold and his life flashed before his eyes, including just how right it had been making love to Alayah. His gaze darted left and right, looking for any way out of this room, but all the exits were tied up if he couldn't reach the stairs. Doing that would likely result in a bullet in his back the moment he turned to run.

"What's happening here, Salma?" he asked, backing toward the stage slowly. If he could drop down in front of the first row of chairs, they might give him cover while he ran.

"Don't pretend like you don't know," she hissed, advancing on him to eat up the distance between them. Not what he wanted. He had to keep her talking and pray she didn't come any closer. He needed help, but from what he could see, he was on his own.

On his own.

No, he wasn't. He had the SOS button Cal had given him the night Ryland had brought him to the hotel. When Cal explained all of their clients were given one, he'd felt unexpected relief. Cal considered him someone in need of help and not the monster Detective Henry had made him out to be. Not that he'd ever thought he'd have to use it, but here they were. All he had to do was figure out a way to activate it. The trick was to get his hand down to his pocket without Salma noticing.

"I honestly wish I knew," he said, hoping to keep her talking. "Obviously, it has something to do with Hugo."

She mocked him, repeating his words while tossing the gun around in the air. He used her moment of distraction to slide his hand down his side to push the button. At least, he hoped he'd pushed it. He couldn't risk Salma thinking he had a gun.

"Hugo had to go. It was that simple. Once Hugo was gone, we could take the company public and actually be paid for our hard work."

"Who is 'we'? You and Curtis?"

"Ha!" she exclaimed, the sound harsh in the giant space. "Curtis is a wimp. A windbag who wants to act like the boss but could never be the boss. He doesn't have the balls to do the hard jobs when they arise."

"Like killing people?" he asked, moving closer to the row of seats. "Does he know what's happening here?"

"Do I look stupid?" she asked, taking another step toward him. "Telling that patsy would have been a surefire way to have the cops at my door."

"I'm confused, Salma," he said, keeping her talking. "Once Hugo was dead, did you send those guys after me? I don't understand why you needed the app files when you already had access to them."

"We searched for the files, but since it was Hugo's little pet project, he must have decided he didn't want to share. When we couldn't find them, I knew you'd have a copy, so sending my men to get them and take care of you, killed two birds with one stone. I got the file and you were dead. Well, you were supposed to be dead. I told them to go in and make it look like a robbery gone wrong, but those idiots couldn't even do that. Here's a tip. Never hire untrained felons. Thankfully, I got them out of police custody before they talked." She checked her watch. "Too bad they won't survive their final ride. Now, it's time to take care of you, which has been harder than I anticipated since you hooked up with another team. Didn't see that one coming, but no matter, I'll take out the trash and be on my way."

"Josh." He said the name in hopes of getting a reaction from her. When her lips tipped up in a smile, he had his answer, but to keep her off balance, he dug in for the story. "Was he blackmailing you?"

"Such an annoying little gnat," she snapped, pronouncing the *g* the same way Hugo used to, before she giggled mercilessly. “Hugo was right about that boy. He was willing to do anything to get that app, so it wasn’t hard to convince him to join me with the promise of selling it to him.”

“You mean he wasn’t blackmailing you?” Derek asked, catching movement from the corner of his eye but forcing himself to stay focused on Salma.

“Blackmailing? No.”

“I don’t understand why he had to die then, or was that an accident, too?”

“Like you, he had to die to get him out of the way. He was already making noise about stepping into Hugo’s shoes at Black Marlin and merging our companies. There wasn’t a chance in hell I’d ever let that happen, so he was another mess I had to clean up. Thankfully, he was driven by greed, so it wasn’t hard. You, on the other hand, have annoyed me beyond measure.”

“You know this entire room is covered in cameras, right?”

She waved the gun around so wildly that he feared it would go off. “Usually it is, but darn, those cameras went down at just the wrong time. When they come back online, the fun will be over. You’ll already be dead, and I’ll be long gone.”

“Wrong,” a voice said from behind him and his blood ran cold. The movement he saw must have been Alayah sneaking through the side door. Why would she put herself in danger rather than alert the Secure One team? He desperately searched for a way out. “I know you’re here, and I won’t let you hurt Derek.”

Salma scoffed. “Such a touching tirade from someone barely able to reach my kneecaps. Forgive me if I’m not shaking in my boots.”

"Alayah," he hissed, stepping to the side to shield her from Salma. "You need to run."

"No," she whispered. "Distract her."

Distract her? He could only think of one way to do that. "Do you know who Hugo left the business to?"

"To the board, of course. He knew we'd protect his legacy from poachers."

"That's why you killed him? So the board could take the company public?"

He dropped his hand and Alayah nudged it with hers. Was she trying to hold hands? That's when he registered the cold metal she slipped into his palm. A gun. This brave woman put her life in danger to bring him a gun. When they got out of this room, alive, he was going to ask her what she was thinking and then tell her just how much he loved her.

"He made it clear that wasn't going to happen until he was dead. It felt like a gauntlet thrown, so I stepped up because Curtis wasn't man enough to do it. I'd hoped they assumed you'd done it, of course, and then, once you were dead, that would be the end of it. Instead, here we are."

"Here we are indeed," he said, a grin splitting his face. He noted it made her nervous, so he kept it up even as he moved in front of Alayah to prevent her from getting caught in any crossfire. "Hugo lied to you. He didn't leave the business to the board. He left the entire business to me. After this, I'm afraid I'll have to fire you."

"Big talk from a guy not holding a gun," she said before dropping her arm.

"Get down!" he yelled to Alayah as he raised his gun, the look of surprise on her face the last thing he saw as he pulled the trigger. He dove to shield Alayah as a loud retort filled his ears and pain blossomed across his chest.

"Stay down!" a voice behind him yelled, and then another pop and loud bang filled his ears as people started yelling about ambulances, and the hall flooded with light.

“Derek!” Alayah screamed.

“Stay down!” Cal yelled. “Her gun is still hot!”

The next thing he knew, Alayah was leaning over him, holding something to his chest as she screamed for help.

“Hang in there, Derek,” she begged, leaning down near his ear. “You’re going to be okay. The hospital is practically across the street.”

He lifted his left arm, the only one he could move, and ran his finger down her cheek. “If I don’t make it, know that I’ve fallen head over heels in love with you, Alayah.”

She put her finger to his lips as her eyes filled with tears. “Don’t say it. You just think you’re dying, which you aren’t, dammit! We can talk about this when you pull through. When you pull through. Do you hear me?”

“When,” he agreed, nodding weakly. “When.”

Chapter Twenty-Six

Alayah stood outside the hospital as the sun rose over Lake Superior. It held a whole new meaning this morning as she replayed the events of the last few hours through her mind. By the time the ambulances arrived, Selina had stabilized Declan, one of her Secure One colleagues, who had been shot in the leg by one of Salma's wayward bullets. Derek had taken a bullet to his chest, and while it looked bad, the doctors had assured her it wasn't life-threatening. Unfortunately, it had to be removed to prevent it from migrating into his lung.

I've fallen head over heels in love with you, Alayah.

Derek's proclamation had been playing repeatedly in her head since they'd wheeled him away from her. She was too small to keep up with the stretcher, and Selina had held her back so she wouldn't get hurt trying to. It wouldn't be long, and she'd be allowed to see him, but she was still no closer to knowing what to say than she'd been in that convention hall. Did she feel the same way? Absolutely. Could she ask him to adjust his lifestyle to meet her needs? She hoped there was a compromise in there somewhere, but she also knew that was a lot to ask of anyone who suddenly had too many unexpected decisions to make about his own life.

She inhaled deeply again and watched as the sun warmed

the lake, raising clouds of smoky fog into the air. There was always something magical about early mornings over the lake that let your soul rest.

"You don't have to have all the answers right now," Selina said, and Alayah started in surprise.

"How long have you been there?"

"Long enough. I remember being where you are and wondering if the man I'd fallen in love with, against my battered resolve, I might add, would want to live the kind of life I now had to live. It's heavy."

"Truer words," she agreed. "I'm not sure I'm strong enough to carry it, and that's really the crux of the problem."

"Is it a problem for Derek, though?"

"That's my exact conundrum."

Selina shrugged. "It didn't look like a problem to me when he was refusing to let go of your hand despite the EMTs trying to keep him alive."

"That's different. That's trauma," she said, leaning on her walker that Selina had insisted she bring to the hospital. In fairness, it was a lot of walking, and she was exhausted. "Asking someone to sign up for life is entirely different."

"That's valid, but not allowing them to make their own decisions isn't fair."

"What if he doesn't choose me?" She'd finally voiced the question that had run repeatedly through her head for days.

"What if he does?" Selina asked, patting her back. "Do you want to miss out on a love story because of the unfounded fear of getting your heart broken? Only you can answer that question, but Derek should get a say in it when he's so obviously falling hard for you."

She shook her head as she gazed at the lake smoke. "Life isn't normal for him right now. He might cling to whatever safety net he found, mistaking it for love when, really, I was grounding him in the tornado that had become his life."

"I recommend you open your eyes before walking into his room, Alayah. Open your eyes and see what the rest of us see. Did you ground him? Absolutely. Your giant heart grounded him and showed him that sometimes love happens at the most unexpected time and place. The only emotions you can control are your own. You can't tell him how to feel. All you can do is listen and decide if his emotions echo your own. Only then can you move forward."

Alayah nodded, her shoulders drooping as she turned away from the sunrise to face the hospital again. "How's Declan?" she asked to change the subject as they walked back inside.

"The doctor is ready to talk with us about his surgery."

They hurried down the corridor to the family room and entered to see Cal, Efren and Roman pacing the room while Zac sat in the corner, shell-shocked. His elbows were propped on his thighs, and his hands were buried in his hair. Alayah wasn't sure he was even breathing.

She walked to him, jumped up on the chair beside him, and rubbed his shoulder. "He's going to be okay," she promised, but it didn't seem to filter as he stared at the wall, unmoving.

A man in surgical scrubs walked through the door and closed it behind him, drawing everyone's attention. "I'm Doctor Jokela, an orthopedic surgeon who cared for Declan. He gave me permission to speak freely with everyone. After consulting with a vascular surgeon, we were able to stop the bleeding and repair the vessels damaged by the bullet."

"That's good news," Cal said with a nod. "Is there a but coming?"

"Unfortunately, there is," the doctor said. "As with most

injuries that we see from a hollow-point bullet, the damage to his leg was catastrophic. It obliterated his hip joint and shattered his pelvis. We had no choice but to perform a hip disarticulation with repair of the pelvis."

Alayah felt Zac's sharp breath under her hand, but otherwise, he never moved.

"You're standing in a room full of amputees," Cal said with a nod. "We'll take care of him. What are the next steps?"

"He'll need time for the pelvis to heal before anything can be done regarding a prosthesis, if he chooses to go that route. As you know, some hip disarticulation amputees find value in a prosthesis, and others prefer a wheelchair or crutches. For several months, it's my recommendation that he use a wheelchair to protect his pelvis from reinjury. Physical Therapy will recommend a plan to maintain his strength, and Prosthetics will begin discussing options with him. The most important part for now is healing the pelvis fracture and giving his vasculature time to recover."

Cal nodded once. "Anything he needs, he gets."

"He's out of surgery and in his room, but still relatively out of it. It's my understanding you've had a long night, so please feel free to go home and rest. He'll be in good hands here. You can call and check on him at any time. Mr. Newfellow, we have your number for emergencies."

Cal nodded, but Zac stood, stalking toward the doctor. "I want to see him."

"As I said, he's still sleeping off the anesthesia and may not know you're there."

"As I said, I want to see him," Zac repeated, his teeth clenched as Cal gripped his shoulder to hold him back.

"Zac—"

"I'm the reason he's in that bed," Zac said, cutting him

off. “I failed him last night. He will not go through this alone.”

The doctor, obviously confused and uncomfortable, opened the door. “I’ll let the nurse know you’d like to see him. She’ll notify you when he’s settled.”

“Thank you, Doctor Jokela,” Selina said with a nod. “And thanks for taking good care of our friend.”

“From what I’m told, you’re the reason he made it to the hospital without bleeding out, so I can say the same to you. I’ll be checking on him over the course of his stay here, but I trust that you’ll take the lead on his outpatient requirements?”

“Absolutely,” she assured him. With a nod and a wave, he disappeared down the hallway.

Everyone in the room turned to Cal and Zac, still locked together in the center of the room. Cal had both of Zac’s shoulders now as Roman walked over and put his hands over Cal’s from behind Zac. Efren stood on his left side and Selina on his right. Alayah had seen them do it multiple times while working at Secure Inc. Selina had explained that it was their “no one left behind” box. It was meant to remind the person struggling that they had their back and every side.

“The only person responsible for Declan being in that bed is sitting in a jail cell,” Cal said, his voice stern but kind at the same time.

“It was my job to watch his six, but I failed, Cal. You should fire me on the spot. What good am I if I can’t keep my brothers safe?”

“Zac, we all understand what you’re feeling right now. We’ve all been in your position where we felt our failures were the reason for someone’s injury or death. It will take time for you to see what happened in that hall with emotional detachment, but it will come. When it does, you'll see that you didn't fail Declan. You read the situation and followed your instincts when you pulled him down. Had you not done that, he'd be dead. That bullet would have hit center mass and we'd be in a morgue instead of a hospital. Everyone in this room knows that. I promise that when the drugs wear off, Declan will say the same thing. Your feelings are valid, and we're here to support you as you work through this. Every person in this room loves you, and we all know you'd step in front of a bullet for any of us. That's the reason you're on and will remain on my team. Hooah?"

"Hooah," Zac whispered, his face crumbling as he dropped his forehead to Cal's shoulder while the rest closed rank around him.

"Hooah," Alayah whispered, suddenly knowing what she had to do.

Chapter Twenty-Seven

When Alayah reached Derek's room, she heard talking, so she paused outside the door. She'd wait there for them to finish and use the time to take some deep breaths and remind herself of what Selina had said. Derek had the right to make his own decisions, and she had to respect that. The conversation inside the room reached her ears and she paused.

"What happens to Black Marlin Technologies now?" Derek asked someone.

"It's a real mess," the man answered, and she recognized Anthony's voice. "I'll straighten it out while you recover, so don't fret about it. Salma sang like a jailbird once they offered her a reduced sentence to come clean."

"She told me most of what she'd done while we were in the hall."

"Did she tell you that she was having an affair with Josh Hunt?" Anthony asked.

"What? No, she said he wasn't blackmailing her, but he was too up in her business about the app, so she got rid of him."

"As the lawyer for the business, I'll get to read her statement, but from what I understand, she claims they were partners in their endeavor to take control of Black Marlin Technologies."

"Considering how hard he was working to get the app from Hugo, I would buy that. Why'd she kill him?"

"Salma claims it was an accident."

"Blunt force trauma to the head is always an accident, right?" Derek asked sarcastically.

"It's not my monkey, but I would guess it will take many months of tracing their movements to find the real truth."

"I'm worried the rest of the board knew about her plan," Derek said, but that was one thing Alayah was certain wasn't true. The odds that four people would all agree to this plan didn't work for her.

"From what I could ascertain, they didn't, but Minneapolis PD is questioning them as we speak. I'm confident they'll seize computers and records until they're happy Salma was the only culprit here."

"I'd be lying if I said it wasn't a struggle to wrap my head around it. Both what she's done, and that the company is now mine," Derek said weakly. Her heart clenched. Alayah wanted to run to him but didn't want to interrupt his visit. She'd wait for an opening. "The saddest part is that two men are dead because of her greed. Hugo was a good man, and while Josh had his issues, he didn't deserve to die."

"Agreed on all accounts," Anthony said. "The only immediate suggestion I would make on the company's behalf is to offer the other three board members a severance package and cut ties with them."

"I need someone there who can run things while I'm recovering," Derek said.

Alayah's heart sank. He was going back to the city. She'd suspected he would, but she hadn't anticipated how painful it would be to hear it confirmed.

"We'd bring in a tiger team to keep the company running and the employees on task. They're experts in this type of situation, and I'd be there to oversee it as well. You would be in the loop via video and phone until you recover enough to return to the office."

"What if I don't want to return to the office?" he asked, and Alayah's heart stuttered to a stop momentarily. "The idea of returning to the city and jumping back into that life, the life that killed a man I cared deeply about, has lost its appeal."

"Then you don't return to the city," Anthony said, and she noticed him shrugging when she moved closer to the open door. He had his back to her and blocked Derek's line of sight, so they didn't know she was there. "You own Black Marlin Technologies. If you want to move it somewhere else, do it. If you want to sell it, do it. If you want to hire someone else to run it, do it. I'll help you sort it all out, but Hugo would never want his gift to become a burden."

"Thanks, Anthony. I want to continue running Black Marlin, but I want to do it from a little house where I can see the lake in the morning as the sun rises, and a beautiful woman in my bed every evening as it sets. Is that asking too much?"

"Not in my book," he said, turning to see Alayah at the door. He smiled, motioning her in. "Speaking of beautiful women, one is here to check on you, I'm sure. I'll let you two talk, but I'll be back later once I get a handle on Salma's confession."

Anthony shook Derek's hand, and then, with a wave, he left them alone. She approached Derek's bed and noticed a chair beside him with a stepstool and booster seat in it.

"Hi," he said, a weak smile on his face. "I'm glad you're here."

"Hi, I'm so happy to see you awake and talking. Is this for me?"

"The nurse assured me you'd be able to hold my hand in that contraption," he said as she climbed up into the chair. When he slipped his hand through the railing, she grasped it tightly. His right arm was in a sling against his chest with a pressure bandage under his hospital gown. "Looks like she was right."

"I've never been so scared as I was last night," she whispered. "I'm glad you're going to be okay."

"What you did tonight was ridiculously brave, but you shouldn't have put yourself in danger, sweetheart. Did Cal read you the riot act for bringing me that gun?"

"Not yet. He's been focused on Declan, but I'm sure it will come. I did what I did and have no regrets."

He nodded, his gaze drifting to the ceiling. "They told me about Declan. Distraught is the only word I can use to describe my feelings. His life has been changed irrevocably because of me, and that doesn't sit right."

She wanted to placate him, but she wouldn't. He would have to come to terms with what happened in his own way, and she'd support him in any way she could. She dropped his hand and moved the stool over to the side of his bed, using it to climb up and sit beside him on the left so she didn't hurt him, before she wrapped her arms around him. There was no talking, just comfort offered and accepted in the face of a traumatic and terrifying situation.

After a few minutes, he kissed her forehead and sighed heavily. "The moment you wrapped your arms around me, my pain slowly ebbed."

She turned her face to his and smiled. "I'll be here for as long as you need me to be."

"So forever then?" he whispered, dropping a kiss on her

lips despite an oxygen tube in his nose and machines beeping all around them.

"Forever?" she squeaked, his gaze so intense she wondered if she'd combust from the need building inside her. "What about Black Marlin? I don't do well in the city, but if that's what you want, we'll find a way."

"The only thing I want is a quiet place to enjoy my life. Hugo's life and death taught me there's no time to waste when true happiness is within reach."

"You're saying..."

"I'm saying I love you and want to spend the rest of my life with you."

This time, her heart stuttered in a wonky rhythm of hope and fear that left her struggling to think of the right things to say. "I love you, too, but I can't ask you to stay," she said, tears falling down her cheeks. "My package is small and complicated."

"And beautiful," he whispered, kissing her again.

"It might take you the rest of your life to convince me of that," she said, her lips tipping upward as her heartbeat switched into a new rhythm of hope, love and anticipation.

"If that's what it takes, then I'm in," he promised. "Together, we can face any storm. We've already proved that to the universe this week. And before you say it, I'm not feeling this way because we've been in a state of trauma since we met. The moment I laid eyes on you, my soul settled in a strangely uncomfortable way."

"That's encouraging," she muttered, which got her a muted chuckle.

"What I mean is, everything fell into place. Every piece of my life I'd been struggling with moved into position, and the picture of my new life came into view."

"Like a soulmate?"

"How does that sound to you?" he asked.

"Like something I don't deserve but want all the same," she answered honestly.

"Then let me be the one to prove to you that you deserve the world. You're the hero I didn't know I needed, Alayah. I love you."

"I love you, too," she whispered, pressing a kiss of forever to his lips.

* * * * *

Don't miss Declan's story
the next installment in Secure Watch,
the new Harlequin Intrigue miniseries
by Katie Mettner
On sale November 2026,
wherever Harlequin books and ebooks are sold.